About the Author

Kim Bergsagel lives in Edinburgh and is a passionate artist, puppet maker, yoga teacher and flamenco dancer. Kim visits India regularly to train in yoga and lived for a time in Ahmedabad, Gujarat, with her husband, Symon Macintyre and their two children, Rachael and Ewan. When not writing, she can be found in her studio or walking her dog Felix on the beaches of East Lothian.

Indy Monroe

Kim Bergsagel

Indy Monroe

Olympia Publishers
London

www.olympiapublishers.com
OLYMPIA PAPERBACK EDITION

Copyright © Kim Bergsagel 2024

The right of Kim Bergsagel to be identified as author of
this work has been asserted in accordance with sections 77 and 78 of
the Copyright, Designs and Patents Act 1988.

All Rights Reserved

No reproduction, copy or transmission of this publication
may be made without written permission.
No paragraph of this publication may be reproduced,
copied or transmitted save with the written permission of the publisher,
or in accordance with the provisions
of the Copyright Act 1956 (as amended).

Any person who commits any unauthorised act in relation to
this publication may be liable to criminal
prosecution and civil claims for damage.

A CIP catalogue record for this title is
available from the British Library.

ISBN: 978-1-80439-489-2

This is a work of fiction.
Names, characters, places and incidents originate from the writer's
imagination. Any resemblance to actual persons, living or dead, is
purely coincidental.

First Published in 2024

Olympia Publishers
Tallis House
2 Tallis Street
London
EC4Y 0AB

Printed in Great Britain

Dedication

I dedicate this book to Symon Macintyre; I couldn't ask for a more supportive life partner who, very importantly, still makes me laugh.

Acknowledgements

Thank you to my husband, Symon, who has put up with my obsessive plot rambles. Thanks to my manuscript readers, notably Melissa, Lisa, Ingrid, and Anne, who gave helpful advice. A big thank you to Revanta Sarabhai for giving me invaluable advice on Hindi and Gujarati. Thanks also to my niece-in-law, Emmi Bergsagel, who has served for many years as a flight attendant and who refused to let me stray into an impossible territory, and, lastly, huge thanks to all my friends in India for responding to my endless questions.

Chapter 1
Glasgow 2018

The man's body hurtled through the glass window at breakneck speed like a stone smashing through an icy lake. Splinters of glass cascaded towards the watching crowd that had been jostling to catch a better view, testing the rope cordon which had been placed in front of them. However, with the onslaught of a dead body heading towards them amidst a shower of debris, there was an audible gasp as the crowd retreated backwards, causing an element of panic.

A loudspeaker penetrated the ensuing chaos. "Please keep calm. Keep calm and no one will get hurt."

Heads craned to get a better look at the body which lay at an awkward angle, head twisted to one side, legs splayed, one arm crooked behind its back, the other thrown over its head as if to protect it.

There was a gasp, then a rumble amongst the crowd as they struggled to get a closer look. Was this an accident or deliberate? Had something gone wrong? What was it they had witnessed?

One of the security guards on cordon duty turned and shouted, "You can all go home, the show's over."

Authoritative theories abounded as the crowd began to disperse. A few remained at the cordon and watched as a woman approached the body and crouched down to examine it. She was slight in build, her black hair pulled back into a sleek ponytail and she wore a figure-hugging skirt suit. Her eyes surveyed the limp body and then came to a stop. She leaned forwards and let out a startlingly raucous laugh, then stood up, her hands automatically smoothing the tight skirt over the curves of her body.

"Sorry, but you might want to take a look at this."

Robert, the floor manager, approached her, his lips talking into a small microphone at the corner of his mouth, his eyebrows raised in question. She gestured towards the man on the ground and he stifled a giggle.

"Ken, I think you'd better get down here." He winced at the response in his ear and then shrugged his shoulders, throwing her a beaming smile.

They waited silently and then watched as a well-built man in his fifties strode towards them. He had a shock of thick white hair, and an equally striking thick black moustache. His eyebrows were lowered over his humourless, piercing blue eyes which never wavered from the body. He reached Robert and quickly glanced at him, then followed his eyeline down to the corpse.

"Bloody hell, the bum's showing," Ken's deep voice boomed in rich, round vowels. He put his hands firmly on the area of his hips, though his hands failed to gain any purchase due to the increased expansion of his waist over the last twenty years, and exhaled loudly, clearly conveying his exasperation. Reaching down, he tugged at the corpse's trousers, then stood up and tugged at his own, lifting them firmly back into place. He swore again.

"I told Katie to fix them on properly. For Christ's sake, what the hell is going on? I mean it's pretty bloody obvious that the force of getting chucked through a window is going to put a strain on the clothing. Can't anybody do anything properly around

12

here?" Ken had an imposing manner that left you in no doubt on meeting him that he was a director of one of the most successful Netflix detective series.

Robert looked at his watch and then raised a megaphone to his mouth, "OK, everybody, take five."

John, the production manager and Ken's general dogsbody, trotted towards the director. He seemed flustered and nervously approached the group, looking glumly at the bristling moustache, his eyes darting from one figure to the other. He winced as Ken's voice enveloped him in a booming tirade.

"Well... you idiot, don't just stand there! How did it look? Go and check the playback, and make sure it's OK. I don't want to have to shoot it again, but on the other hand we can't have Detective Inspector McKinley's final body lying arse to the sky with its pants down.

"After all, this is the last episode. It's meant to have the audience begging for more, not laughing the house down."

As John hurried off, Ken stood up and with some obvious effort kicked the dummy corpse over with his boot. It rolled with an unnatural twist to face upwards, revealing to those close enough to see a glassy-eyed stare at the sky above.

The lingering onlookers exchanged a mixture of curses and "I told you so's" to one another. A few even threatened to sue the film company for trauma for not telling innocent bystanders that they were about to witness a fake accident.

Indy Monroe sat in her trailer. She looked, quite literally, like she had died. A great wound opened across her cheek bone, her nose was flattened and dried blood dripped over her forehead and down her face. Rachel, the makeup artist, smiled at her.

"Fantastic. You look great."

Indy grinned back at her. "I can always rely on you to make me look good."

"Don't smile, the latex is still drying." She leaned in with her powder brush and began to blend the outer edge of the wound into the skin.

Looking directly ahead of herself into the mirror, Indy watched her as she worked. "It's a good job. I look very dead. Detective Inspector McKinley, the final episode—"

"Indy, please…"

"Sorry!"

"Ken will give us a bloody rocket if we have to delay the last shot. Especially after what just happened with the corpse. Let me finish."

Indy looked at the mirror in front of her and stared at Rachel. The bulbs beaming out light from around the outer edge were harsh, giving her a strange pallor despite her all-year tan. Over the last six years, Rachel's appearance had changed. Previously blonde-streaked hair which had once been casually swept back in a ponytail was now a vibrant copper-coloured bob, neatly blow-dried and held in place with industrial hairspray. When they had first met, Rachel was a youthful woman in her late thirties; now, she was an attractive woman in her early forties who was very careful with her appearance. The skills used for enhancing features for film and TV were applied each morning no matter how early the call time. Indy liked Rachel. They had established a gossipy, girly banter that occasionally stretched to meeting for a night out drinking, which invariably meant being unable to move the next morning. Rachel caught her eye, and returned her stare with a concerned expression.

She furrowed her carefully plucked eyebrow and whispered,

"Is this really the end of DI McKinley?"

Indy opened her mouth to talk, but stopped when Rachel frowned and tutted, squirting a blob of blood into the wound. She shrugged and the makeup artist continued, carrying on the one-sided conversation.

"What I don't get is that if the ratings are still high, why does nobody know whether there's a new series in the offing? I heard that the controller has changed again and we've got someone called Daisy Yates now. Do you think she will really axe a successful series?"

She stood up and took one last look at Indy, double-checking her work, then whipped away the protective cloth from Indy's costume. *"Ta da!"*

Indy looked at the bloody reflection in the mirror and said, "I've been DI McKinley forever. When I was thirty, I thought, wow! What a lucky break, no money worries; I've made it! Six years later, I wonder if I can do anything else. Maybe Detective Inspector McKinley is the only part I'll ever play? So the conclusion I have come to is that whether it's the end of the series or not, this is my chance to have a breather, take some time out for me and find out who Indy Monroe really is."

Rachel looked at her and saw that beneath the scarred tissue, she was serious.

Indy laughed. "But then again, give me a few months and I might be crawling back broke and desperate to be McKinley again." She touched her cheek absentmindedly, touching her new scar, then caught Rachel's expression. "Oh, sorry, I forgot."

Rachel leaned forward to check for damage, turning the seat to face her, then swinging it back to view her work in the mirror again.

"The only shame is seeing the whole team breaking up,"

Indy continued once Rachel looked satisfied.

They stared at each other through the bright reflection. Indy broke the brief silence. "So, what's next for you then?"

"*Aha*, thought you'd never ask. Just another couple of well-paid jobs to go and the cat is in the bag so to speak! By the time they get this show on the road again, I'll look 30 and have the perfect hourglass size 10 figure."

Indy grinned as best she could within the constrictions of her prosthetics. She had become used to Rachel's botoxed lips being unable to smile for at least two days each time they were done. Rachel's aim was to leave nothing to chance when it came to her face and figure.

Indy didn't share the same vision, but each to her own. Her eyes smiled. "You going to the wrap party?"

"I wouldn't miss it."

They were interrupted by Robert throwing the door open.

"Come on, ladies. I'm trying to keep Ken calm after the dummy's Bum Incident as I call it. The crew's on double time to get this shot in so let's get moving, shall we?" He closed the door behind him with a flounce and Indy and Rachel exchanged glances.

"They love you really," Rachel said as she grabbed her basket of tricks and stepped out the door of the trailer. Indy sighed, took one last glance in the mirror and followed her.

Chapter 2
Glasgow 2018

The film company had booked the Arches for the wrap party and invited every known body that the series had ever seen. The place was transformed for the night. Set dressers and scene shifters had been working hard, turning the alcoves into replica sets from the series. The game of the night was to try to remember who did what to whom, in which episode and from what series.

By midnight, the congratulatory speeches had been made, and after many claps on the back, hugs and kisses, the crew and the actors had divided into groups. Wine and beer were still flowing, and the debris of food and snacks lay around like clues for Hansel and Gretel.

Nobody was going home early.

Members of the crew squeezed into the set of The Pole Dance, an early case that involved Detective Inspector McKinley discovering the remains of various exotic dancers left in suitcases in Govan. It was the best place to keep an eye on the dance floor and had the advantage of being only a short journey to the bar to stock up on pints of beer.

The music throbbed and the coloured lights pulsated to its rhythm in the dark, cavernous room, while sweaty, scantily dressed women writhed around the dance floor, in what they hoped was a provocative manner. The men did their best too, shifting from foot to foot, lifting a shoulder or an arm, in the hope that these actions, combined with an occasional lean or two of the body, would convince people that dancing was practically second nature to them. It didn't, but on the whole, people were too inebriated to care.

Indy had placed herself on the edge of the Situation Room, series 3, episode 2, which was full to bursting with the regulars from the series. Dawn, the pretty blonde PC was in a clinch with Jeff, the Dangerous Cop with the Drug Habit.

Having exhausted the continuous barrage of questions as to her future career prospects, Indy stood on the edge of the dance floor, drink in hand. The spotlights that were focussed on the tables glared a beaming light, casting the people sitting around into semi-darkness, so that if you half-closed your eyes, you could almost imagine a dance of dislocated hands moving glasses and bottles up and down, in and out of pools of light.

A deep voice interrupted Indy's reverie and pulled her attention round to face Ken who was looking relaxed, having completed the shoot. Tonight, he had put all work problems behind him. Editing would start soon, but for now he had his gin and tonic and a smile on his face. It was good to see.

"So, where will you be this time next week?" he asked.

Indy sighed and then tossed her head back to look up at the director's face with a grin. "India. I'm flying into Mumbai. My plans are loose, but I'll see what I can, moving up to Delhi, Agra, the Taj Mahal. You know, the important bits. I might take a trip to Goa, I don't know. I don't feel like tying myself down to a schedule, not after six years of film shoots! It's hard to believe, but I've never been there before."

Ken smiled. "Sounds great. Will you be looking up your relatives? Where are they from again?"

"Gujarat." Indy smiled. "I don't know. It would seem the logical thing, wouldn't it? But I've never met them, so it feels a bit strange. They didn't approve of Mum's marriage to my dad; marrying a heathen bum, you know!" She laughed ruefully. "I'll see how I feel. I don't speak Gujarati, and for all I know we wouldn't be able to communicate anyway." She turned her eyes away from his gaze.

Ken put his hand on her shoulder. "We'll miss you. Six years is a long time. I've got used to seeing your face day in and day out." He cleared his throat and blustered forcefully, "You'd better make the most of your break. Mark my words, the series isn't over yet. Daisy may think that she is making her mark by clearing the decks of the established programmes, but Detective Inspector McKinley will rise again to solve another case."

Indy rested her hand gently on Ken's arm and smiled up at him. "I'll miss you too; especially your shouting!" she teased. "But series or no series, we'll keep in touch."

Ken stroked his thick moustache absentmindedly, caressing the ends towards a point and twisting. The effect was mildly comical, creating a lopsided cavalier style look. He stared at the floor. "Have you talked to Angus?"

Indy raised her eyebrows in surprise. She hadn't anticipated the question and no one yet had mentioned his name despite the fact that this was the first time they had been in the same room together in almost a year after a very public marriage followed by an equally public divorce. She shook her head, biting her lip while she formulated an answer, something that would explain or justify her unwillingness to move forward. The truth was she still hurt and at this moment in time, she needed to ignore his presence. Ken nodded and gave her a sympathetic squeeze. Tears sprung to her eyes and she removed herself gently, mumbling incoherently.

Her heart raced as she fought back the turbulent emotion that was boiling within her. she attempted to calm herself as she manoeuvred herself through the hot, sweaty bodies towards the ladies toilets. Avoiding eye contact so as to discourage attention, she kept her head down as she forged her way through all these people she had worked with all these years. The technicians, actors, set designers, sound engineers and the others who had watched her day in and day out on set. She had been their focus throughout and she felt their mixture of celebration and sadness tonight.

A strong hand gripped her arm, preventing her from moving forwards. She turned, unwilling to have to make light conversation just now and froze momentarily as she found herself looking into Angus' face. His expression had a joyous innocence as if he was genuinely pleased to see her and fully expected her to feel the same way. But his face clouded over as she looked at him and he carefully removed his hand from her arm. She stared at him wordlessly.

He sidled towards her, leaning in close in order to make his voice heard over the din of music and people. She felt his breath caress her skin and smelt the familiar odour of Noir Extreme. She used to buy that for him. She used to revel in its fragrance.

"It's good to see you," she heard him saying, "you're looking well."

Indy shook her head. No, he wasn't going to be allowed to be nice to her yet. Not yet. It was too soon. Her eyes swept the crowd and she wondered which young up and coming actress he was with tonight. At her party. She settled on a slender young blonde with a skin-tight short dress. She didn't care if he was with her or not, this girl would do. This girl would enable Indy to rekindle her anger and revive the memories of all his infidelities.

She arched an eyebrow and stared hard at Angus, enjoying

his uncertainty, fixing her eyes on his, willing him to look away first and then turned abruptly away from him.

Angus let out a slow sigh, grinding his teeth as he shook his head slowly while he watched her battle her way through the crowd. He had been delighted to get an invitation to the wrap party and had genuinely been looking forward to seeing her. But this meeting quickly reminded him of the gulf between them and made clear that the old wounds were still unhealed. Indy could annoy him in a way that nobody else could. Excite him and annoy him. He folded his arms around his chest, clenching his fists, his body tense. The throbbing, pulsating music wrapped itself around him as though it were trying to gain entry into the fortress his body had become. A figure jostled past him and he felt the gates open, releasing him from the frustration that had taken hold of him momentarily. He was here, damn it, and he would enjoy himself whether Indy Monroe liked it or not.

Chapter 3
Goa 2018

Indy lay in a hammock, her soft hat perched over her forehead, shading her from the hot sun. A book was in her hands, but she was having difficulty focussing her attention on the story of life in the Arctic. Life just seemed too good in the sun.

She revelled in the relaxed ambience of Goa and had found the state a welcome respite from the demands and excitement of the rest of India. Initially, she had been a little concerned about whether she would feel comfortable travelling on her own, but this experience had shown fellow travellers she met to be welcoming, whether they were single, in pairs or in groups. She had discovered the unexpected delight of solo travel, being able to suit oneself without having to accommodate anybody else. She could read when she wanted, walk when she felt like it and there always seemed to be somebody around with whom to exchange ideas or share the experience of a trip to a market or temple. She could enjoy their company and part without further demands.

Indy had been in Goa for two weeks now. She had flown into Delhi and had spent a few days wandering the busy city seeing the sights before joining the mass of tourists, moving on to the must-see Golden Triangle of Agra, and Rajasthan. The Taj Mahal was indeed truly breath-taking and she had made a point of following the advice given in her guidebook of being there to witness the sun rise and set. Seeing the pinks and oranges of the sky sweeping across the white marble had been a photographer's dream and her phone was crammed with postcard-worthy shots. India was overwhelmingly crowded with people, teeming with vigour, colour and noise. It was bewildering and invigorating and exactly as she had expected while at the same time being a complete surprise.

Indy was aware that she felt a need to try to imagine what her mother's life was like growing up in this country. She knew that as a child she had repressed her fascination for India due to her embarrassment at being ethnically different. She had endured the small-minded racism in school that had invariably reared its ugly head and it had made her want to negate her Indian origin. According to a great many people who were more than happy to share their opinions, she had achieved a successful career either 'despite' being half-Indian or 'because' she had minority status. After six years of being DI McKinley, she could afford to shrug those comments off, but a part of her wondered if that was why she hadn't ventured away from the role.

Either way, she felt she had a greater understanding now of what a shock it must have been for her mother to move from India to a small village in the highlands of Scotland. A wave of guilt swept through Indy at the hurt her rejection of her Indian identity must have caused her mother.

She swung her leg out over the edge of the hammock onto the ground, kickstarting it into a rocking motion and lowered the book onto her stomach, leaning her head back onto a cushion. Things would be different when she got home, she mused, and she looked forward to being able to share her experiences when she saw her parents. A shadow passed over her and she opened her eyes, smiling in delight at the beautiful Indian woman standing by her side.

"You're blocking my sun, Sonal," she joked, raising her head to speak.

The woman moved to one side, casting a glance at her position regarding sun and shade. "I think it is not necessary for you to have more sun on your body. You are already dark enough. You should be careful."

Indy rose to examine her skin and sighed, swinging her body out of the hammock, and landing lightly on her feet.

She laughed. "It is a mystery why some cultures are sun worshippers and others spend their time avoiding the sun."

"A mystery you cannot solve…?" The woman flashed a wide smile, revealing a perfect set of even white teeth.

Indy threw her companion an uncertain smile. She was aware that the reference to solving mysteries was due to her fame as DI McKinley. She had been astonished to have been recognised regularly throughout her trip, with perfect strangers directly accosting her, or giving her disconcerting stares or not-so-indirect glances. She was used to it, of course, at home, or even in Europe, but in a country so far away, both geographically and culturally, it had taken her by surprise. However, although occasionally annoying, she had to admit that on the whole it was flattering to be noticed and whispered about. She hadn't felt so alone. In fact, she had met Sonal and her husband, Prakash, due to her role as McKinley. It turned out that Sonal was an ardent fan of the Netflix series and, Indy suspected, seemed to have some difficulty separating the two characters. Initially, when Sonal had made reference to her various crime-solving abilities, she had made a point of correcting her, clarifying fact from fiction. But over the short period of time they had known each other, she sensed that it was more complicated for her friend. It became clear to Indy that Sonal invested in her fictional life to deal with her reality. She seemed to have a need to believe in Detective Inspector McKinley. Indy realised that this could be seen as worrying or alarming, but in Sonal the result was sweetly charming. And after all, what harm could there be in the mild delusion?

She lifted a rumpled piece of cloth from the hammock and wafted it in the direction of the sea, letting it drift slowly down to the sand. Smoothing it slightly at the edges, Indy gestured Sonal to sit down beside her.

"Where's Prakash?" she asked, shading her eyes from the sun as she turned to look at her friend.

Sonal made sure her broad-brimmed hat was creating as much shade as possible, arranged her dupatta to cover her arms, and tucked her feet under her. She frowned and answered, "He is walking. He likes to walk, you know, regularly, many times a day. At home, he goes to the gym. Here, he walks."

Indy looked at her and hesitated momentarily. "Don't you like to walk also? Why don't you walk together?"

A flicker of something indeterminate crossed Sonal's face and she turned to look at Indy squarely.

"Are you happy?" she asked.

Indy was unnerved by the unexpected question. She stammered her response, "Well, I'm not unhappy...I mean, I'm mostly happy I suppose..." She swallowed hard. There was an overwhelming sadness that wrapped around the words of this question. A sadness that reached out towards her and seeped into her pores. It was as though over a cup of tea, an acquaintance had suddenly and unexpectedly revealed herself to have an empty void within a beautiful shell.

"Are you...not happy? Why do you ask?"

Sonal stared at her. "I no longer know what happiness is. I live. I exist. I have food and a big house. I have a husband and a child. But happy?" She shook her head.

Indy furrowed her brow. "But why?" she enquired. "Was it an arranged marriage? I'm sorry, I don't mean to be rude."

Sonal lifted her arm and flicked her hand as though waving away a fly. "No problem, I am not at all offended. My marriage was arranged in that we were formally introduced, but I could accept or not as I wished."

Indy looked surprised. Sonal smiled, and then her smile faded. "Prakash was nice and very charming, with a good job. I liked him and agreed to marry him. After the marriage, we moved in with his parents. They have a big house and at this time I think I could say I was happy."

She stared into the distance above Indy as if to ponder what she had just stated.

"Yes." She nodded. "At this time, I was happy. But three months later, I discovered that he was in love with another woman and had been in love with her before he even met me. In India, this is a breach of contract to say you are free when you are not. I was very angry and I decided to take him to court to divorce him."

Indy looked at her in astonishment, aware how little she knew about the marriage arrangements in India, then said, "But you are not divorced. What happened?"

Sonal sighed. "What I was doing was very serious and at the same time I discovered that I was pregnant. Prakash told me that his relationship with this other woman was over. He told me he would buy another house, just for us so that I would not have to live with his parents. They were very angry at what I was doing and I didn't want to live with them any more. I was persuaded – I decided – not to divorce him." She lowered her eyes.

"So what is the problem? What has gone wrong?"

Sonal's face took on a hard, cold sadness. "Prakash bought another house, but he works long hours. It is hard for me to be on my own all the time. When he is not working, he is at the gym or…elsewhere. My daughter must see her grandparents and Prakash likes to see them too. I think he feels more comfortable around them. So we spend most of our time staying at their house and not ours. We have no time together."

"But you are here together now. He is holidaying with you," Indy stated as though this fact negated what she had just been told.

"This is the first time we have taken a holiday away from his parents and my daughter. Prakash says he is trying to save our relationship. But he walks. He walks without me." Indy bit her lip. "I'm sorry," she muttered. "I wish there was something I could do to help you."

Sonal stared hard at Indy, locking her with her eyes.

"You can help me. I think my husband is still seeing this other woman. You must follow him and find out where they meet and tell me. I must know." Tears began to fill her dark eyes, until they spilled over, pouring down her cheeks. Indy scanned the face in front of her and it occurred to her that if looks equalled happiness, Sonal should be swimming in it. She reached out and gently took hold of Sonal's hand.

"I am not Detective Inspector McKinley," she whispered. The woman in front of her showed no sign of response.

"I am not a detective, I am an actress. This is not a job for me," she insisted, her voice imploring Sonal to listen and understand what she was saying. Sonal's eyes hadn't left Indy's face.

"You will help me. I need you to find out if my husband is seeing another woman. You can do this for me." She rose as if to signify that their meeting was at an end, leaving Indy to stare helplessly after her.

Chapter 4
Calicut 2018

Prakash peered out of his open-fronted shop, scanning the bustling street for a sighting of Indy. He had sent his car to fetch her, but he knew it could take a while for it to reach him. It would have to negotiate its way down a road filled with large, highly decorated trucks and carts pulled by bullocks. The street teemed with merchants and traders organising the loading and off-loading of huge sacks of spices. Bare-chested men, with immaculately pressed cotton shirts worn like un-buttoned jackets, wafted the bottom corners of their mundus and kyleys, cooling their wiry brown legs, before tucking the long fabric up into the waist where they tied the cloth to form a simple, short wrap.

Prakash sat down on a crate and pulled out a cigarette from the top pocket of his perfectly ironed short-sleeved shirt. He tapped the end lightly before placing it between his lips and smoothing down his moustache, then he lit the end and inhaled deeply. He was looking forward to welcoming Indy to the Spice Market and his shop. His father had been a spice merchant as had his grandfather and Prakash knew this business like the back of his hand and he loved it. He remembered hanging around the shop as a boy, chasing the mice as they scurried across the huge sacks filled with pungent aromatic spices such as cloves, cinnamon, turmeric, cumin… He had known that one day this little empire would be his and it gave him a feeling of huge importance. The spice trade had a history that went back thousands of years and his ancestors had been intrepid travellers in search of the highest-quality ingredients. This remained one of the most enjoyable perks of his business, travelling round the world, tasting and trading spices. He was looking forward to showing off the results of his endeavours to their guest.

The smoke oozed through his teeth and out of his barely parted lips and he crossed his legs, one hand resting on a knee, the other reaching upwards to support his head. He rubbed his forehead abstractedly, his thoughts drifting to his wife and he frowned. These days he steeled himself to go home. The place was as inviting as a mortuary, and as far from the atmosphere of the house he had grown up in as you could get.

He jumped with surprise as a hand tapped him lightly on the shoulder. Indy was standing over him, dressed in an orange and blue kurta pyjama outfit stitched with small pieces of mirror, that sparkled in the sunlight, looking every inch the Indian woman.

"Welcome." He smiled, leaping to his feet and gesturing for her to enter the premises. Prakash's shop was not designed to entice the average domestic purchaser through the door. Its sole purpose was the trade market. Huge sacks of spices piled high stood ready to be delivered by road, sea or air to shops throughout India and abroad. The interior was essentially an old-fashioned warehouse, dusty and dark, but Prakash beamed at Indy with the pride and excitement of a king showing off his palace. He led her towards some large sacks standing in the centre of the back room and plunged his hand into the nearest one to him, holding out his palm for her to inspect. She stared at it, unsure of what to say.

"Go on, smell it, taste it. What do you think?" he grinned.

She bent over his hand and inhaled. The aroma was intoxicating. The few spices she owned which sat on the poorly stocked spice rack at home were tasteless and insipid compared to these rich, evocative and sensual aromas. There was a fresh and pungent quality that took her by surprise. She took a piece of what looked like bark from the palm of his hand and bit into it uncertainly. Prakash watched her intently, encouraging her to continue. Indy's eyes widened with surprise. It was cinnamon. But cinnamon the likes of which she had never experienced before.

"This is gorgeous," she murmured. "The flavour is so intense."

Prakash nodded. "Chinese," he proclaimed, waggling his head enthusiastically. "In most cases, I would say that India produces the best of everything, but with cinnamon I would have to agree that Chinese has the greatest flavour." He looked at her, pleased that she had been so appreciative.

"Here, have some more."

Indy helped herself to another piece with a grin, glad that she had honestly been able to do his spices justice, though she felt that a little cinnamon went a long way. Mice scurried along the tops of the produce stacked around the room and she vaguely wondered as to the hygiene issues of what she was eating and indeed on the implication of hygiene for spices in general, before dismissing these thoughts as, under the circumstances, pointless speculation.

Prakash led Indy back to the shop front, and, calling authoritatively for one of his staff to bring a chair, he flourished a handkerchief over it in a gesture of cleanliness and motioned for her to sit down. She obeyed. Prakash was a bundle of nerves, a mass of nervous energy. "Coffee or tea?"

"Masala chai, if that's possible," Indy answered.

"No problem," Prakash responded with a waggle of the head, "anything is possible." He turned his gaze back to the crowded street and lifted his chin, his eyes darting from left to right, finally alighting on their target and shouting aloud, he waved his arms to attract attention.

The chai wallah came running, a young lad armed with a kettle filled with hot, spiced, milky sweet tea which he poured deftly from the spout into a small cup, plucked from an array of cups that jangled around his thin body. She received it gratefully and Prakash nodded, tossing a few coins into the boy's palm. He perched himself nervously on the edge of a box and crossed his legs. They sat in silence for a while, Indy sipping her tea, glad of something to do. Neither of them had spent much time together and this experience of being in each other's company without Sonal was a rare one.

He cleared his throat. "I am very happy that Sonal has found such a good friend."

Indy smiled. "Thank you, Prakash. You have both been very welcoming to me." She paused, waiting for him to continue, but he fell silent. Seeking to fill the awkward silence, she said, "She is very beautiful."

He raised his eyebrows. "You think so?"

She stared at him in surprise, almost shocked at this indication of disinterest in Sonal. "Surely you must know that?" she persisted.

He looked at her. "You may have noticed that my wife and I…we do not…" he trailed off and she waited for him to continue.

Prakash brought his fingers together in a gesture reminiscent of thoughtful prayer, and tapped them together slowly.

"May I speak freely?" he enquired, his eyes fixed earnestly on hers.

She nodded, taken aback by the prospect of an intimate conversation. "I married my wife in good faith and voluntarily. But I had been in a relationship with another woman who I loved very much. I wanted to marry her, but she was very modern. She wanted a career as a flight attendant and was not ready to settle down. I felt that it was time for me to marry. I have my shop, my business" – he gestured to the premises – "and I needed to start a family. I need to pass my business on to my son."

Indy looked at him and wondered if his daughter was as inconsequential to him as his wife appeared to be.

"So we agreed to part so that I could make my marriage arrangements. But during my engagement with Sonal, Arundhati contacted me saying she had had second thoughts about my proposal. I was confused, I didn't know what to do. To break my contract with Sonal was unthinkable, but my desire for Arundhati was…I am very much ashamed to say that we had a brief relationship again." He paused in thought, before drawing himself up to continue. "But I finished the affair before I married Sonal."

Indy observed Prakash sitting cross-legged in front of her. There was an air of pomposity about him, and she wondered idly why he was sharing these intimate details with her, but she found herself mildly intrigued despite herself and smiled encouragingly for him to continue.

He shifted from side to side and kneaded his fingers together. "I am very sorry to say that Sonal found out about Arundhati. After we were married. I was a fool. I had printed out emails from her to keep them – like letters. I couldn't bear to throw them away. They were in a box and the dates showed clearly that I was…that we were…"

Prakash lifted his eyes to hers and his expression was distraught.

"Ever since then, we have lived as though we are apart. I have tried to make her happy but it is no use. Nothing I do seems to please her. I think she hates me now."

"Prakash." She paused, trying to choose her words carefully. "I am not a marriage guidance counsellor. I am not sure why you are telling me this."

He shifted in his seat, his bare foot twitching his sandal between his toes nervously. Waggling his head with great emphasis, he gestured towards her in a beseeching manner. "I want you to help her, to be a good friend to her. She needs a friend. It is not good for her or for any of us that she is unhappy. I don't know what to say to her; she locks me out of her life now. Please be there for her. We need you."

Indy considered him. It seemed that both halves of this couple were imploring her to get involved in their relationship. She had never thought of herself as someone with any particular skills in helping others and she couldn't help but be flattered by their belief in her. It wasn't what she had come to India for, but maybe this was better than a holiday of sheer indulgence. There was something mildly exciting about playing Lady Bountiful with a touch of Detective Inspector McKinley thrown in for good measure. She saw herself as in a film, having successfully brought them back together, waving magnanimously to the happy couple who stood arm in arm on the doorstep of their house with their child nestling between them and she smiled at this vision.

Prakash cleared his throat. "So, you don't mind me speaking to you in this way? You will stay with us for a while and be a good friend to my wife?"

Indy re-emerged from her reverie and blushed slightly. "I'll stay for a bit, Prakash. I can't promise anything."

He grinned at her, his head jiggling enthusiastically. "No problem. We are very happy that you are staying with us. Very happy indeed." He rose from his seat with great agility and clapped his hands. The car honked its horn in acknowledgement of the signal and Indy realised the interview was over.

Chapter 5
Antwerp 2018

Indy stepped out onto the pavement and zipped up her coat. A gentle breeze rippled her hair and she took a deep breath, filling her lungs. The air in Antwerp felt thin and clear, a sharp contrast to Calicut with its hot, humid thickness and pungent smells. In India, she had revelled in the soft, loose clothing, but now there was an exotic thrill to feeling her body pressed into close-fitting jeans and long-sleeved tops. A young woman passed her, her decorated dreadlocks gathered upwards so that they fell like a plume around her face. She wore a long skirt swirled with embroidery and a thick padded Tibetan-style jacket fastened with ribbons. A cacophony of colour on a street filled with variations on a theme of dark.

Indy smiled, enjoying the cultural reference to the East. She was looking forward to exploring it further on her return.

She reached into her pocket and pulled out the piece of paper Sonal had given her, containing a note of the hotel in which Prakash was staying. Sonal had explained that Prakash had told her he was on a trip to meet a potential investor in his spice business, but when questioned further, he had become very vague. This had aroused her suspicions and much to Indy's surprise, Sonal had paid for Indy's flight and accommodation to Antwerp.

Indy had waived any additional costs on the basis that Sonal's obsession was already creating a huge hole in her bank account. In any case, she was worried about Sonal and was keen to put Sonal's mind at rest. Hopefully for good.

She typed Prakash's address into her iPhone and watched the pulsing blue dot appear, indicating her location, and set off. Genius. It would be a pleasant walk in the late winter sunshine. A few people in their coats and jackets sat at tables outside cafes, drinking coffees and eating pastries. She crossed over a bridge underneath which wound the canal. Market stalls were just setting up, a sprinkling of people – perhaps dealers – hovering for that first bargain of the day. In other circumstances, she would have enjoyed spending time leisurely watching life and browsing the market, but this morning she had her mission and she was compelled to focus on her route, her eyes darting obsessively from phone to immediate surroundings. She was close. She stepped out onto the road and was confronted by a jangling of bicycle bells and shouts because she had looked to the right automatically. India, like the UK, drove on the left and she hadn't had to acclimatise to the change in direction of traffic. She lowered her phone in order to concentrate on crossing the road and narrowed her eyes. She had reached her destination. An Indian man in dark, neatly pressed trousers and a grey anorak over a brown jumper was walking rapidly along the pavement across from her. The way he moved reminded her strongly of Prakash, but she couldn't quite see his face from her angle. Keeping to her side of the road, she scurried quickly in the same direction, trying to dart ahead of him in order to get a good look at his face. It was Prakash. He turned left away from her and she raced to the traffic lights, hopping from foot to foot as she waited for the signal to cross. He had disappeared. Her eyes scanned the view ahead, searching for the slight figure. Thankful for her foresight in wearing trainers, she managed to run swiftly across the road, weaving between pedestrians, finally catching sight of him just as he reached the hotel.

The street was busy, with an army of bicycles passing in each direction, but opposite was a tree-lined park where she noticed an empty bench. It seemed a good place to pass the time and she settled down to wait.

She had brought a book in an attempt to look inconspicuous, but it was hard to concentrate on the story and she found her eyes repeatedly flickering over to the building in case she missed Prakash. She was glad to see him finally emerging. He was hunched, his arms hugging his chest, his head moving furtively from left to right. She pulled the hood of her coat over her head and instinctively sank down into the bench in an attempt to disappear. It was obvious he was scanning for observers but even from across the road, she could tell that his eyes were wild and there was little chance he was absorbing what he was seeing. He passed a rubbish bin and she saw him reach into the pocket of his jacket, looking furtively from left to right, before taking an object out and then throwing it inside. Allowing him just enough space to move on, she crossed the road, weaving between the bicycles, and reluctantly reached her hand into the bin, her fingers grasping something hard and rectangular. To her surprise she pulled out a phone, but there was no time to examine it because as she glanced up she saw Prakash disappearing ahead. She gathered speed, cursing as she tripped over a paving stone, the phone slipping out of her hand. She picked it up, giving it a quick once over to see if there were any obvious signs of damage and was relieved to see the screen was unbroken. A tall Indian-looking man with a well-manicured beard bumped into her, apologising as he passed, but she looked away, thrusting the phone into her pocket, and scanned the street ahead for signs of Prakash. She could just make out his grey anorak ahead and she propelled herself forwards, narrowing the space between them until she got close enough to keep a careful distance apart. She followed him back to his hotel where he stood outside for a moment before disappearing into the building.

Indy stood outside the entrance trying to understand what had just happened. Had he been visiting a client on business as he had told Sonal? But why had he thrown away a phone? She shook her head in thought and wondered, not for the first time, what she was doing here in Antwerp when she should be enjoying a holiday in India.

Looking around her, she felt her senses opening to the sounds and smells of the city. She had never been to Antwerp before and this was her chance to explore the tourist destinations.

Perhaps the jigsaw pieces would settle into the puzzle more easily if she took her mind off the 'Prakash Case' for a while.

It was time to see the sights.

Chapter 6
Antwerp 2018

Indy lay in bed. She had endured a fitful night's sleep and she pulled herself up to a sitting position with effort. She dreaded the day ahead. She needed to come to a decision about whether to go to Prakash and ask him straight up if he was having an affair with Arundhati. Then she could tell Sonal and get back to her holiday and put an end to all this cloak and dagger stuff. She leaned over and reached for her bag, dragging it onto the bed. Rummaging around inside, her fingers sifted through the contents, eventually finding their quest. Prakash's phone. She pulled it out and looked at it. Why had he thrown it away? She stabbed at it in the hope that it would magically open, but knew that it was useless. It probably needed either finger recognition, a pattern or a sequence of numbers and Indy had no idea what those would be. Birthdays were the most likely, she mused as she tossed it onto the bed. She headed for the shower and turned it on full and cold. Stepping inside, she let out a gasp as the torrent of water hit her body. Her eyes opened wide and every nerve seemed to blast awake. She swivelled the dial to red and felt herself slowly relax as the warmth cascaded over her. She knew what she had to do, there was no choice. She had to face Prakash and let him know what she had been doing on behalf of Sonal. He would be angry, but it might give him the chance to end the affair – if he was still having one.

She dressed swiftly and walked down the stairs to the

reception desk. The man behind the counter welcomed her with his usual smile. "I hope you have a nice day, ma'am," he said as he accepted the key from her with his extraordinarily long fingers.

Indira returned the smile, her gaze drifting down towards his hands that were resting on the daily tabloid newspaper. A large photograph of an attractive Indian woman peered out from beneath his thumb and forefinger and she furrowed her brow, moving closer to get a better look. He moved his hands away to accommodate and whistled softly between his teeth.

"A terrible thing," he murmured. "She looks quite happy in the photo. Still, you never know what goes on in people's lives, do you?" He tutted, moving his head slowly from side to side.

Indy's eyes scoured the page, vainly trying to gain an insight into the story. "What happened?" she asked, an unsettling feeling pervading her body. If this was what it felt like to get a premonition, she was having one now.

His eyebrows rose and his eyes widened with surprise. "You have not heard? A terrible murder. It seems an Indian woman was killed in a hotel not far from here. A flight attendant with Qatar Airlines. They haven't got the killer yet, but…" He looked up and saw the effect his story was having on her. Indira had turned pale, all colour drained from her face and he ceased talking for a moment to stare at her. "Don't worry, Miss, I'm sure you're quite safe." He searched momentarily for a theory which would sensibly explain what had happened. "I expect that it's probably a drug deal or something."

His face showed concern for his guest and he gestured for her to sit down.

Indy shook her head. "What was her name? The girl who was murdered." She held her breath as the receptionist quickly

39

scanned the article.

"Here it is, A…" He stumbled over the syllables, eventually arriving at an approximation of the name. "Miss Arundhati Adani."

Indy closed her eyes and nodded. She had known the answer before he had said the words, but when he spoke the name 'Arundhati Adani', she felt her insides dissolve.

She had to go somewhere where she could think. Somewhere where she wasn't being scrutinised by an over-attentive receptionist. She managed to throw a wan smile in his direction and murmured about being late for an appointment, then turned towards the door. As she walked across the lobby, she felt her body trembling and it took all her powers of concentration to move one foot in front of the other to exit the building.

The sky was blue and the sun's rays warmed her face as she stood on the pavement. Bicycles whizzed past her and people went about their business as though nothing had happened.

There was no doubt in her mind that Prakash had killed Arundhati, but why? It was obviously too dangerous to confront him now, but what should she do? Go to the police? She shook her head. Nobody knew she was in Antwerp, let alone that she had seen Prakash enter and leave the building and she would like to leave it that way. She had been stupid to get involved anyway. She grimaced. Sonal. Much as she would like to walk away, she owed it to Sonal to tell her…what? That her husband was a murderer? Indy bit her lip. Maybe she would just have to tell her that she had failed to find out anything; as she had said to Sonal in the first place, she wasn't a real detective. Arundhati was dead so maybe that would mean that Prakash would come home and the two of them could live happily ever after… Prakash the

Murderer. Indy shivered.

She tried to focus on what she should do but her thoughts were muddled and she couldn't follow a single thread that made any sense. She was aware that she was moving forwards and had left the hotel. Where was she going? Where could she go? She closed her eyes tightly and shook her head as though to clear her brain.

Putting one foot in front of the other, she walked, not caring where her feet were taking her. She usually found walking perfect for problem-solving and right at this moment, she was grateful for something to do. She didn't know where she was going and she didn't care.

Mentally, she repeated the words the manager had said. "A terrible murder. A drug deal perhaps. Arundhati Adani. Arundhati Adani…" Indy came to a stop and looked across the road at a modern business hotel, its name written in large red letters across the frontage. She realised that she was staring at the letters, and was aware that subconsciously her brain was scanning them over and over, but the connection from subconscious to conscious hadn't yet occurred. There was something about this name that resonated. The information swirled inside her brain and then slipped into place. This was where Prakash was staying.

Without a thought of what she would do if she saw him, Indy crossed the road, narrowly avoiding the swarm of bicycles flowing past her. She was about to step through the entrance door when she saw Prakash approaching the reception desk. She turned swiftly and peered through the large glass frontage that gave a clear view of the hotel foyer. Thank god for modern architecture. The very tall, blond manager was handing him what looked like a bill, which Prakash signed, rummaging in his wallet to find a credit card that he then placed in the card reader. Indy felt her heartbeat race. It looked like Prakash was leaving imminently which meant she had to come to a quick decision as to what to do. She watched him thank the manager and call for the lift. As soon as the doors closed on him, Indy took a deep breath and stepped into the lobby.

Smiling brightly at the tall blond man, she rested her hands on the front desk. "Hi, I wonder if you can help me. Do you speak English?"

Piercing blue eyes gazed down at her disconcertingly. "Of course, madam. How can I help?"

"Well, I hope this doesn't sound silly, but I was wondering if you could give the man who was just here a message from me? I want to invite him to dinner tomorrow."

The man's face remained impassive. "Madam, the man just paid his bill. He is leaving tonight for Mumbai." He waited for her to absorb this piece of information and then said, "Would you like me to call his room so you can speak to him?"

Indy shook her head vigorously. "Oh, no, no, thank you. I...*um*...obviously got the wrong idea if he is leaving so soon. I feel a bit embarrassed. Thanks, thanks all the same."

She turned to leave, then had a thought and turned back to the tall man. "I don't suppose you know which airline he's taking, do you?"

"That would be confidential information I couldn't possibly reveal," the man answered with a sniff.

"Of course," Indy murmured, feeling frustrated that she couldn't flash her police badge and order him to speak. Things were so much easier in fiction. However, there was another alternative that was often used in scripts and in reality-though she had never personally tried it. She rummaged in her bag and pulled out her purse, discreetly taking out a note, hesitating, then

42

on reflection adding another and gently slid them onto the counter towards him, her hand resting lightly on top.

"You have been so kind, I wonder if there is anything else you can think of that might be of help?"

Quick as a flash, the note disappeared like magic from beneath her palm and behind the counter.

"I believe Air India is quite a popular airline to take when travelling to Mumbai," he said, his face expressionless and impassive.

Indy smiled, then nodded, "thanks again. There's no need to mention I stopped by. It was obviously my mistake."

She turned on her heels and walked out of the hotel. Her heart was pounding, but she felt elated. It had worked! She exhaled deeply and gathered her thoughts. So it seemed he was leaving in a rush. She had time to change her own flight and catch the same one as Prakash. She quickened her speed. So this is what she was going to do then. Follow Prakash and see what was round the corner…

Heading back to her hotel, she approached the reception desk with urgency. "Is everything all right, ma'am?" Franz enquired with a look of concern.

Indy nodded. "I have to leave for India tonight," she said apologetically.

Franz' eyebrows furrowed. "I hope it is not this murder that is sending you away so quickly?" he enquired in a sympathetic voice.

Indy threw a reassuring smile at him, and shook her head, "Oh, no! It was a bit of a shock, but no. A friend of mine is getting married and you know Indian weddings are very big occasions. There's a lot to do and I have offered to help out." She paused. "I wonder if you could help me?"

"Of course, ma'am. Which city were you wanting to go to?"

"Can you see if there is a seat on an Air India flight this evening to Mumbai?" she asked.

Franz nodded. "But of course. I will call you once I have some information for you." He smiled.

She smiled gratefully and headed for her room.

Chapter 7
Mumbai 2018

Indy stood in the pre-paid taxi queue at Mumbai Airport and pondered. She was tired. It had been a long night and a restless one on the flight from Antwerp. She never slept well on planes at the best of times, and this was not the best of times. She wasn't sure why she was continuing this charade, playing detective, and yet there was undoubtedly part of her that couldn't walk away from the events. The unanswered questions, the unknown story. She wanted to know what had happened and knew that for the time being, she was incapable of moving against the stream of events or stepping aside to watch the action carry on without her. She needed answers – not for Sonal – but for herself.

Indy had tried to keep Prakash within sight during the journey, without being seen by him. This hadn't proved too difficult during the journey. Most people wrapped themselves up in blankets and tried to catch some sleep. She had stayed behind him as he left the plane, and had managed to follow him through passport control. Unfortunately, when they had arrived at the baggage collection area, Prakash had picked up his luggage before her, and by the time she had collected her suitcase, he had disappeared.

Indy frowned. She hadn't wanted to call Sonal just yet. Not until she had a clearer idea of what Prakash was up to in Mumbai, but now she would need some help to find him. She vaguely remembered Sonal writing down the address of a flat Prakash kept in Mumbai, but off hand she had no idea where she had put it. She pulled out her Indian mobile phone and keyed in Sonal's number. She needed to find Prakash.

The phone rang and Sonal's voice answered, but it was a recorded message. Indy sighed in frustration. She would have to find somewhere to stay, rid herself of the suitcase and try again later.

It was eleven a.m. Mumbai time when she sank into the back seat of the pre-paid taxi heading to her accommodation.

"First time in India?" The driver's voice broke her thoughts.

"No, well not quite. First time in Mumbai," as if to explain.

"Very nice city," he continued. "Many things to see. Let me give you my card. I can take you to very many places, whatever you want to see, I can show you. What are your plans tomorrow?"

Indy frowned. She had forgotten what it was like to be on the receiving end of one of a billion people needing to make a living. The relentlessness was exhausting however much she admired the persistence. She understood, but right now it was the last thing she needed.

She accepted the card graciously. "Thank you. I can't go on a trip tomorrow, but I will call you if I decide to see something in Mumbai."

"No problem, ma'am. My name is Sandeep, you call me on that number anytime and I will give you a very good rate."

Indy caught sight of his face smiling broadly at her in the rear-view mirror and smiled back at him despite herself.

"Thank you, Sandeep." Indy sighed, glad to have averted one hassle so easily. She slid the driver's card into her wallet. *You never know,* she mused, *it could be useful to be able to call on someone after all.*

Indy felt sweat trickling down her skin, between her breasts and underneath her arms. Mumbai was a contrast to Antwerp in all ways; heat, noise, traffic, numbers of people, smells and pollution. Black smoke exuded from exhaust pipes as buses, rickshaws and scooters headed towards each other, swerving and nearly missing miraculously. It was like a giant game of dodgems with pedestrians thrown in for good measure.

She reached for her mobile and scrolled down until she came to Sonal's name and touched the call button. Still no answer. Indy frowned and placed the mobile back in her bag.

A good rest at the hotel had cooled her quest. Under the refreshing shower of cool water, the past twenty-four hours had seemed like a ridiculously manic pursuit from which she would be wise to step away.

She looked around her and saw she was near Le 15 Café, somewhere that offered an unchallenging environment in which she could enjoy some refreshment and gather her thoughts while offering respite from the heat. The décor was trendy, earthy wooden floors and tables contrasted with dainty black and white chairs, a place designed for middle class Indians and tourists. A counter displayed an array of enticing cakes and pastries and Indy settled onto a cushioned bench, welcoming the cosmopolitan offerings.

Her bag vibrated and a Bollywood tune emanated from her bag. She had been delighted when Sonal had recommended the tune; a 1970s famous popular hit that had felt like a gift from India and she had made it Sonal's personal ringtone. Her stomach flipped as she realised that she was unprepared for how to phrase the news that she had decided to end playing at being detective. She rummaged in her bag and pulled out the gold encrusted phone – another fun afternoon with Sonal. She had laughed as

Sonal had picked out phone case after phone case with brightly coloured, bejewelled ornaments, or photographs of famous Bollywood stars and even cute pink animals, and presented them to her with delight, a far cry from her normal choice of plain black or at a stretch, blue. A scrap piece of paper fluttered down onto the table along with her phone and she caught it before it fell onto the floor.

There was nothing for it, she would just have to be firm – nice, but firm. Pressing the button, she held the mobile to her ear. "Sonal!" she answered brightly. The noise of public announcements blared in her ear. "Sonal?" she repeated. "Hello, Sonal, it's Indy."

It was a pocket call. A woman's voice could be heard in the background and Indy could just make out that a flight was leaving for Delhi, and another saying there was a delay to someplace else she had never heard of. She pressed the red button to end the call, wondering what Sonal was doing in an airport and where she was going. Her tension eased as she realised that at least it meant that she wouldn't have to tell her the bad news. Not yet, anyway.

Indy fingered the piece of paper absentmindedly. There was something familiar about the texture of the paper and the way it was folded and she opened it, curious to clarify the memory. The writing was round and flowed in curvaceous circles in red ink. Indira closed her eyes. It was Sonal's handwriting and the words were her husband's name, Prakash, with the address of his flat in Mumbai. She leaned back against the wall, staring at the information. Why had this piece of paper revealed itself now, just when she was planning to step away from any further involvement in this couple's marriage. She liked Sonal, but there was nothing more she could do for her. The piece of paper rotated between her fingers and she groaned. No, she couldn't go there, she mustn't. But even while these words were floating through her brain, she knew that it was too late. The idea had grabbed hold again and for better or worse, she had climbed aboard the ride.

Rummaging in her bag, her fingers found her wallet and she pulled out the card she had been handed yesterday, that proudly pronounced Sandeep to be the most Reliable, Prompt and Honest taxi driver who would drive you anywhere, anytime, for any length of time and distance. She smiled. What more could she ask for?

She rang his number, asking him to pick her up as soon as possible at the cafe. "Will you be wanting me for the rest of the day, ma'am? I give very good rates."

Instinctively, Indy declined the offer and then paused. Coming from the UK, it was hard to get used to the idea that she could afford to have a driver on call, but the truth was, in India it was affordable, and if you could put up with the occasional diversion to their 'friends" shops, it was worth it. She mulled over her plans, such as they were. She needed to get to Prakash's flat, meet with him, and say what? That she had seen him in Antwerp? She shook her head. No, she would ask him what he had been doing and see what he had to say for himself. In any case, she would need transport to get back to her hotel and it would be good to have a taxi waiting.

"That would be perfect, Sandeep," she answered.

Indy stepped into Sandeep's Premier Padmini black and yellow taxicab and settled back in the seat. From the doors to the dashboard and the ceiling, the interior was decorated with colours reminiscent of a psychedelic acid trip. A large male face stared down at her from above.

She leaned forwards towards Sandeep. "I love the decorations inside your taxi. Who is the man on the ceiling?"

Sandeep's eyes widened in the rear-view mirror. "Shah Rukh Khan, ma'am. You must be knowing him? He is very famous, a very very good actor. A Bollywood star." He caught her eyes in the mirror again and stared at her quizzically. "Ma'am, surely you have heard of Shah Rukh Khan? He is the King of Bollywood. Let me play you some of his songs." He reached down to a box beside him and pulled out a CD, looked down to check the label, then inserted it into the slot in the dashboard. A high nasal female voice filled the cab, soon joined by a rich male one joined by Sandeep who sang along, keeping Shah Rukh Khan company word for word, while he negotiated the heavy traffic, beeping his horn and checking his rear-view mirror to see if Indy was appreciating the experience. He seemed satisfied and waggled his head as he turned right, facing the oncoming traffic, then veered across the road to follow the flow of traffic on the left-hand side. She closed her eyes and sank back into seat. Not knowing Bollywood stars was the least of her problems, it seemed.

Indy walked into the grey building and pressed the lift button. Floor number 4. She gritted her teeth. She had little idea what she was going to say to Prakash – if he was even there, but she hadn't been able to redirect her feet away from this path. It was as if she had been pre-programmed to follow the address on the piece of paper and there was nothing she could do about it.

Stepping out of the lift, she searched around for the flat number. The door was a nondescript brown like all the others, and his name was written in small type and placed in a brass holder to the left-hand side. She took a deep breath and pressed the bell, looking furtively around her, suddenly aware that she didn't want to be seen. She took a deep breath. That was ridiculous. There was nothing to link her with what had happened in Antwerp. She was just visiting a friend whom she had met on holiday in Goa. Nodding to herself as if to confirm the truth of her own story, she rang the bell again. A thump sounded from within. It seemed Prakash was in, so why wasn't he answering? She put her hand to the door and to her surprise she felt it open. Slowly, she moved the door away from her and stepped over the threshold.

"Prakash?" she called, her heart thumping as she walked down the corridor, aware that she was tiptoeing quietly, even as she was calling out his name. She gasped as she reached the room ahead, her eyes taking in the furniture that lay tumbled in disarray. Books and papers were scattered in chaotic piles across the floor. The room had been ransacked, it had been turned upside down. She felt panic escalating as she remembered that she had heard a thump which meant that there could very possibly be one of the thieves in the flat with her. She needed to get out of here now.

Indy's scream was stifled by a hand clasping her mouth and a large arm wrapped itself around her waist from behind.

"*Chup!*" a deep male voice said.

She swivelled her eyes wildly, and saw a man with a thin chiselled face leaning towards her, grinning. Episode 4, *The Macleod Murder* sprang to mind. *Scream. Scream!* A strange strangled yelp gasped from her mouth. Irritated by her weakness, she took a deep breath and managed to shift her mouth free, letting out a full-throttled scream.

"Shut up!" the man's gravelly voice shouted, the large hand covering her mouth and nose this time, making it hard for her to find air.

She knew she needed to kick, struggle, fight, bite, but the man was strong and she couldn't gain any purchase. Fear gathered in her bowels as she realised the reality of the danger she was in. How could she have been so stupid? What an obvious ploy – episode 12, *The Mystery of the Lost Souls*. An unlocked, open flat door, with no one answering her calls from the inside – a similar trick of which she, or rather Detective Inspector Zaina McKinley, had fallen foul. She definitely should have known better.

Be that as it may, here she was and given that she was unable to fight her way out, she would have to try reasoning. She willed her body to relax and fought to steady her breath as best she could, trying hard not to think of the many gang rape scenarios… Episode 8—no, she was not going to go there. This was not going to happen to her.

"Scream again and we'll give you something to scream about," the man snarled menacingly. "You understand?"

She nodded as best she could and he slowly released his hand from her face. Indy gasped for air.

"What are you doing at Prakash's flat?" one of the men asked.

Gathering her wits together, she answered, "I came to visit him as a friend. I met him and his wife in Goa a couple of weeks ago. What's this all about?" This last line seemed a bit clichéd and straight from a script, but right now she felt that it fit the circumstance perfectly.

The large man raised his thick black eyebrows. "So you're a friend of Prakash?" He shoved his face towards hers and asked, "Where is it?"

Indy's face showed genuine puzzlement. "Where is what? I

don't know what you're talking about!" She sighed with annoyance at yet another clichéd phrase. Her mind raced to the state of Prakash's flat. "It looks like if you haven't found whatever you're looking for after turning the flat upside down, then it's obviously not here. Why don't you ask Prakash yourself?" She paused. "What is it you think he's done?"

The man stared hard at Indy.

"If you want, we can search you. Thoroughly. That's no problem, is it?" He grinned at his thin companion who moved to the other side of her, both leering unpleasantly, revealing a disturbing array of pink, decaying teeth. Indy's guts did a somersault leap at the threat. What was it they were looking for?

An image of Prakash walking from the hotel in Antwerp played like a film in her brain. She remembered him dropping the phone in the bin and she shook her head as if to clear it. Surely that couldn't be what they were looking for? She hadn't even checked it. "Look, I'm an actress in a Netflix series called DI McKinley. Maybe you've seen it? I'm here on holiday, on a break between filming. I don't know many people in India, and I just thought I would look up Prakash while I was in Mumbai. That's all there is to it, really."

In her experience of scripts, when the captured person tries to appeal to the better nature of kidnappers, unfortunately they don't stand much chance of being successful, but much to her surprise, a huge grin exposed the remains of stained red teeth as the large man next to her started talking with great excitement to his thin friend.

"Vasant! It's the lady inspector! From the TV! Very good series, oh yes, ma'am, very good. *Acha*, I thought I had seen your face before. Detective Inspector! *Ha ha!* Scotland Yard, oh yes."

The thin man scanned her face intently and then exhaled and

she saw his eyes crease in smiling recognition. "Detective Inspector McKinley, I am so sorry I didn't recognise you. What a mistake. Many apologies." He smoothed his hand over his well-oiled hair.

The large man nudged Vasant to one side, jostling himself into a prominent position and said, "*Bhenchod*, yes, a great mistake. Of course, you have nothing to do with this." He too was attempting to improve his appearance by smoothing his hair that was oiled into sculptured clumps on his head. "Let us give you a lift to your hotel… where you are staying?"

Indira stared at the two men, trying to mask the horror she felt at this suggestion. "Thanks," she stammered, "but I have a cab waiting for me downstairs."

The large man persisted, "But it is no problem and it would be an honour to have you in our car. I am so sorry for causing you big problems." His small round eyes bored into hers. One hand rested on his heart, the other was reaching politely, but firmly to her arm, leading her towards the door.

Indy thought hard for a second. Whoever they were, she certainly didn't want to let them know where she was staying, let alone get into a car with them. Reluctantly, she allowed herself to be led down the stairs and out of the building. Her eyes scanned the street for the distinctive black and yellow cab and she saw Sandeep looking at her with a puzzled expression.

She tried to pull her arm from the large man's grasp, but he held on tightly.

"My driver is waiting," Indy heard herself saying and hoped she sounded as assertive as she had intended. "Please let go of my arm."

"But we will take you wherever you want to go and it will cost you nothing—"

"Are you trying to steal my customer?" She heard Sandeep's voice and breathed a sigh of relief. "She has booked me for the day and I have been waiting without payment so far. What are you trying to do to me?" He sounded angry and outraged and the two men loosened their hold on Indy's arms.

She moved towards Sandeep and gave a ghost of a smile, nodding slightly in their direction as she walked away and stepped into the Padmini with relief, settling into the back seat under Shah Rukh Khan's magnanimous smile.

Sandeep turned to look at her with concern. "Trouble, ma'am? I don't like the look of those men."

She returned his stare and shook her head.

"I don't either," she answered. "Thank you for coming to get me, Sandeep. I appreciate it. No problem now, I'll just head back to my hotel, please."

He nodded in response and pulled the car away to the sound of 'Chak de India' on the CD.

It was nearly midnight, and Indy was nursing another glass of rather fine whisky. She hadn't felt up to venturing out into Mumbai this evening and had chosen to eat her dinner in the hotel. A ransacking and a potential assault was quite enough excitement for one day. For a week, actually. Sitting in her hotel bedroom on her large double bed with her feet up, reading a book, whisky in hand seemed the perfect way to wind down and try to relax. Relaxing was the hard part. Indy felt as though her brain was on repeat as she went round and over the recent events, trying to make sense of what had happened. Prakash had had an affair, killed his lover, and then his apartment had been ransacked because clearly somebody was looking for something. But what? And what did this thing have to do with the murder? Had Prakash killed his lover for some valuable object? Obviously not the phone that he had thrown away, but it seemed vital now that she discover how to open it.

She jumped as a Bollywood tune interrupted her thoughts. It was Sonal ringing her. "Hi, Sonal, how are you?" Indy was genuinely happy to hear a friendly voice. "It's late, everything OK?"

"Oh yes, everything is perfect, thank you. Prakash is back home. Thank you for all you did, Indy, it was very kind of you."

Indy hesitated, unsure of how much to say. "Oh, I did nothing, Sonal. No need to thank me."

Sonal continued, "You heard the news, right? That woman was murdered. Well, I knew she was no good. In any case, thank god it had nothing to do with Prakash as he was in Mumbai on business. I don't have to worry about where Prakash is any more. He will stay right here with me."

Indy grimaced, glad that Sonal couldn't see her reaction to the reference that Prakash had been in Mumbai. Was there any way to ask about the phone without mentioning that she had seen him in Antwerp?

"Sonal, I was wondering when your birthdays were – you and Prakash?" she asked, rolling her eyes at the ineptness of this question. It seemed to her so obviously linked to passwords.

On the other end of the phone Sonal laughed. "Our birthdays? Why do you want to know? You have done enough for us, Indy, we don't need any presents."

Clearly the question was only obvious when you had a phone to break into. She sighed.

The memory of the flight announcements from the pocket call re-surfaced. "Sonal, did you take a break somewhere nice?"

There was a pause on the other end of the phone. "Sonal?

56

Are you there?"

"What makes you think I took a break? Why would I be going anywhere? I have been here the whole time."

Indy took a deep breath. "You made a pocket call. You know, by mistake. Your phone called me and it sounded like you were in an airport."

Another pause, and then Sonal said, "It must have been the TV was on. I have been here all day. Where would I be going? *Acha*, it's late and I need to go to bed. Thank you again for all the trouble. Indy, you won't mention to Prakash… anything… will you?"

Indy leaned back heavily against the pillows, and sighed deeply. "No, Sonal, I won't mention anything. Goodnight."

She closed her eyes, folding her lips together tightly. Sonal had just lied to her. A big fat whopping lie. Why? What the hell was going on?

Prakash had lied to Sonal about being in Mumbai when Indy knew he had been in Antwerp, but given that he had probably murdered Arundhati, that was really no surprise. Prakash's flat had been ransacked by two thugs who were looking for something, but she had no idea what or whether it had anything to do with Arundhati. She sighed.

It no longer seemed to matter.

The Sonal/Prakash chapter was closed. They were back together and what she needed to do now was to carry on with her holiday. A smile fluttered around her lips; a holiday. She had forgotten that that was why she was in India.

Chapter 8
Mumbai 2015

Prakash sat back in the armchair, his head resting in his upturned hand, the other arm gesticulating vigorously at the mobile phone in his hand.

"I don't understand what you are saying. I came all this way to see you and you tell me you are not coming? I have gone to a lot of trouble to take time from work and the family to be here. You should remember that."

"Prakash, I am sorry. I can't manage it this time. I am very busy with work. Don't worry, we will make another arrangement. Soon. Just check with me first." A loud smacking kiss followed the sentence and then the phone clicked.

"Arundhati? Hello? Hello?" Prakash stared in disbelief at the mobile he was clutching in his hand and then threw it forcefully onto the bed. He clenched his fists and let out a growl followed by a few expletives, stomping up and down the small room before falling backwards onto the mattress, the phone jamming into his shoulder blade.

Arundhati turned her dark eyes towards the man on whose lap she was sitting and her deep red lips smiled, showing a row of gleaming white teeth. Her long black eyelashes fluttered as she leaned towards him. "There, I am yours only."

Two large hands gripped tightly around her waist and she gasped at his strength.

"You'd better be," the words were uttered with a voice that

sounded like it was scraping the bottom of a barrel filled with gravel. "I don't share my women with anybody. If I catch you with any other man…"

Arundhati leaned in and kissed him on the lips, parting his mouth with hers and reaching in with her tongue to explore him further. He yielded to her probing and she felt her power over him. It excited her.

"Why would I be with any other man when I can be with you?" she smiled provocatively. "Besides, Prakash is just a friend."

Ajay snorted in disdain. "What sort of man stays just friends with a woman like you?" he asked, his lips devouring her neck.

Arundhati moaned as she answered, "A friend who is not interested in women that way."

Ajay's mouth paused as he considered what Arundhati had just told him. He did not approve of homosexuals. The whole concept of a man being sexually interested in another man – himself perhaps – was something he found deeply threatening, and he didn't like to feel threatened. But in this circumstance, he could see no objection to a friendship with a man who was not sexually interested in Arundhati.

He reached under her blouse and deftly undid the back of her bra so that he could ease his hands underneath to feel her breasts.

To his surprise, she pulled back from him and moved off his lap.

"What's this?" he growled.

Arundhati re-fastened her bra and adjusted her blouse. "I am not a prostitute, sir. I don't have sex so easily with strange men."

The heavyset man stared at her, his eyes darkening and there was a pregnant silence while he considered her words. She knew she had taken a huge chance by holding him at arms' length and she held her breath, waiting for the response.

To her surprise and great relief, the man in front of her opened his mouth and threw back his head, emitting a huge guffaw.

"Very good, Arundhati ben. I will wait." He leaned forward. "It seems the first thing we need to remedy then is the 'strange' part." He patted the seat next to him. "Come, have a drink and let's get to know each other."

Arundhati smiled and moved gracefully towards him. He leaned in towards her, his fingers undoing the clasps in her hair. It tumbled down around her face and shoulders, and he wrapped his fingers in the thick, black glossy tresses. Her pulse raced as he lifted her hair and she felt his breath on the back of her neck as he traced his nose along her skin, inhaling her scent.

Her stomach flipped at his touch and she closed her eyes.

"It's been a long day, sir. I flew from Cape Town early this morning and I need some rest." She eased herself away from him and stood smiling at him.

"I must go, but I look forward to seeing you again. Soon, I hope."

"Call me Ajay, Arundhati. If we are going to know each other better, you can't keep calling me sir." He chuckled, his taut round belly bobbing up and down.

Ajay was a big man, approaching six feet in height and his frame was large, although his bone structure was perhaps not as large as the additional pounds he was carrying made him seem. The extra weight was evenly distributed and reinforced his imposing presence. He bore the air of a man used to getting his own way, a man in authority not to be messed with. Standing in front of him, Arundhati felt tiny in comparison and knew that if he wished, he could bend her like a sapling branch. But she was stronger than that, she was a strip of bamboo, tough with sharp edges and eager to reach up as far as she could go. Prakash could never have given her enough, but this man could. She would just have to manage him carefully.

"Ajay," she murmured.

He moved forwards and reached around her, bending over her so that she arched backwards in his arms and this time, he devoured her.

"I look forward to our next meeting, Arundhati," he whispered huskily into her ear. Then he released her and reached for the door.

Two men were lounging in the next room and as the door opened, they jumped up, each placing a hand on his chest in a gesture of respect.

"This young lady wants to go home," Ajay said, glancing at Arundhati, a glimmer of amusement passing his lips. "Get the driver to take her now."

He took her right hand and brought it to his lips, brushing his moustache over it before she felt his moist lips kiss the back of her hand. "Till the next time," he said and turned away, closing the door behind him.

Arundhati collected herself, trying to ignore her heart pounding within her chest and nodded to the men who beckoned her to follow them.

She was on her way up and she smiled at the thought.

Ajay sank down on the sofa with a smile. She was just what he needed right now.

Chapter 9
Ahmedabad 2010

"Arundhati!" A large woman in a flame orange and pink sari sat on brightly patterned cushions that upholstered a large varnished wooden sofa. The television mounted on the wall in front of her blared hit pop songs while women danced provocatively, their hair blown by wind machines as they stared at the camera, pouting, lips slightly parted.

She picked up the TV control and reduced the volume, turning her head behind her. "Arundhati!" she bellowed before turning back and chucking the remote onto the table beside her. "Where is that girl?" she muttered. "Always I must do everything." She complained, turning up the volume.

"You called, Ma?" A slim young woman stood to the side of the sofa, her long sleek hair was worn loose and was immaculately groomed, the ends curling into soft waves. She wore a loose pink t-shirt with a diamante flower design on the front and body hugging skinny jeans with deliberately shredded holes in the knees.

"Where have you been? I have been calling you for ages."

"Sorry, Ma," she answered, "I was in my room and couldn't hear you. Maybe it was the noise of the TV."

The older woman harrumphed and shifted her weight on the couch to turn towards her daughter.

"Your father is asking for you. He wants you to go into the shop and help out for a bit. He has orders coming in today that he needs to deal with." Her eyes scanned the younger woman's outfit. "But what is this you are wearing? Anyone would think we can't afford new clothes. Why must you be dressed in jeans with worn-out knees?"

Arundhati rolled her eyes. "Oh, Ma, they are very fashionable. And why do I have to help Pa out? Hasn't he got someone else who can help him? I was going to see Preeti later on. We were going to the mall."

Her mother shrugged. "I don't know, but he has asked for you." She looked up, annoyed and waved her arm at her daughter, her hand giving extra emphasis with a final dismissive fling. "Go and change first, then help your father."

Arundhati slumped her shoulders in protest.

"And if you don't want to help out in the future, then you had better look at some of the men Auntie is showing you and choose yourself a husband." She turned away with a very definite movement to face the TV and turned the volume up, putting an end to any further discussion on the matter.

Arundhati stared at her, her teeth clenched and muttered at her mother's broad back. "I am not getting married to any old person Auntie brings and I am not going to work in a shop. I'll show you that I can be more than that. I'm going to be Someone. I'll show you, just you wait."

Her Mother watched the flickering screen, oblivious to her daughter's defiant speech. Arundhati turned away swiftly and marched up the stairs to change.

The Adani shop was in Paldi, one of the better neighbourhoods in Ahmedabad. The middle classes had become more demanding over the last few years, and there was a wide range of international products available along with the usual standards. The clientele, with their large cars, often complete with drivers to chauffeur the shopper, indicated that the Adani shop had products that were top of the range or at least desirably

63

expensive. Marmite, mozzarella cheese, parmesan and Betty Crocker cake mixes all graced the shelves – if you knew where to look. The interior of the shop was crammed with goods piled high on either side of narrow aisles.

Arundhati squeezed in through the door, past a tall woman dressed in a beautifully embroidered kurta, sunglasses on her head, perusing the condiments. Arundhati glanced at her father behind the counter who looked relieved to see her and then glanced over at the woman, indicating to his daughter to offer some assistance.

Arundhati waggled her head and stepped forward to start work. Her manner was good with the clients. She was courteous and respectful, but she also had an unusual intelligence in her service that enabled her to anticipate what the client might be looking for, and then suggest another item that might compliment it, or an alternative that could be equally good or even better. People usually left the shop satisfied with their purchases, having bought more than they had intended to buy when they had entered. Arundhati's father knew this and cursed the fact that she had been born a girl instead of a boy – a son who would have taken over the shop, providing an income for his wife and children, and for his parents in their old age. But a daughter? He sighed. A daughter meant marriage, a huge dowry that would probably set him back a few years in debt. He shook his head.

"What's up, Pa?" Arundhati smiled, looking at her father's thoughtful desolation.

He smiled ruefully. "I was just wishing you were a boy." He admitted, scratching his head while he wrote down notes of the last sale.

"Pa! You'll never get anyone better than me. I'll make you proud, you'll see."

Her father's eyes creased and his face softened into a gentle smile as he said, "I am proud of you, my daughter."

Chapter 10
Calicut 2011

Prakash stood in front of the mirror in his room and scanned his appearance. He had chosen a cornflower blue shirt, ironed so thoroughly that there was not a crease or a wrinkle in sight, except for the perfect ridge down the outside of the short sleeves. A dhobi wallah showed pride in one's appearance and a good one was worth their weight in gold. His trousers were neat and belted to show his slim figure, his feet encased in highly polished shoes – despite the heat – and his hair was oiled smoothly into place. He wore a moustache as was the fashion in Kerala. Swivelling from right to left, he checked that all was in place, clean and correct before allowing a slight smile to play around his lips.

He was ready.

Prakash opened the door of his room and ran down the stairs into the large entrance hall of his parents' house. As if by magic, his mother appeared, standing with her hands folded in front of her, staring at him with her black kohl-rimmed eyes. She too was dressed immaculately in beautifully embroidered kurta pyjamas, the tunic stretched over her stout body and the trousers gathered into folds around her ankles, revealing a set of silver ankle bracelets that settled just over the tops of her feet.

"When will you be back from Ahmedabad?" she asked, her hands folded in front of her.

"I have some business to attend to..." he hesitated, then continued, "and then I am seeing someone."

She pursed her lips. "You are meeting that girl?" she asked.

Prakash sighed. "That girl's name is Arundhati, and yes, Ma, I am meeting her. I don't know what is the problem."

Prakash's mother inhaled deeply, rolling her shoulders back to stand squarely in front of him. "The problem is that she is not good enough for you, Prakash. There are plenty of women more suitable than this shop girl. Come with me and I can show you that I have found some very nice, very pretty girls for you to meet." She took his arm to guide him into the living room, but he removed it with gentle firmness.

"Not now, Ma, I have a plane to catch."

"I am serious, Prakash! You can't afford to throw your life away because you see someone pretty who flutters her eyes at you."

"Ma, I like Arundhati. She is not just a shop girl, her father owns the shop. Just as we own a spice business. I am going to meet her and I think if you got to know her, you would change your mind." He placed his hand gently on her cheek. "Please, Ma, don't worry, it's all going to be fine."

Prakash lent forwards to plant a kiss on his mother's cheek and gave her an affectionate tap on her shoulder. She sniffed in response, but allowed herself to be somewhat placated. He was her only son, her pride and joy and as she looked at him, her whole being swelled with admiration at his appearance. He was a man now and she could see he thought he was in charge of his decision making. But she knew what was good for him better than he did. She would just have to think about how to introduce him to the list of women with subtlety – and soon. She sighed as she watched him leave the house and turned towards the kitchen. The maid, dressed in a sari, one end of the fabric looped over her head, was sweeping the floor, stooped over her short-handled sweeping brush. Prakash's mother looked at her, one hand on her hip, the other gesticulating, the fingers splayed out, outstretched and animated, "You are still sweeping? How long do you take? I want my cup of chai in the living room with a piece of cake. Now," and she turned on her heels and left the room. At least, she could control her maid.

Ahmedabad 2011
Prakash pulled up in a rickshaw outside Arundhati's apartment building. It was a modern concrete block of flats, of no particular architectural interest. Demand for housing was everywhere in India, it seemed, with apartment blocks thrown up in the time it took you to walk around the corner. He saw little beauty in this sprawling, dusty city that was so different from his beloved Calicut. Thankfully, his parents' house was in a leafy suburb where there was no threat of overcrowding. He was always grateful to be able to leave his noisy, chaotic spice market, thronging with people, carts and lorries, and come back to a neighbourhood of houses, a neighbourhood with space, peace and nature. The house was set within a garden where he could hear the birds, and when he stepped inside his home, it was cool, light and spacious.

Prakash automatically swept his hair into place. Reaching for his phone, he swiped to Arundhati's number.

"I am here, waiting for you outside. Are you ready?"

She had specifically asked him not to come up for her, despite his protestations that it was the right thing to do; to meet her parents properly and show that he was a respectable man with serious intentions. Arundhati had laughed and told him that she enjoyed having a life without her parents breathing down her neck, and what was the fun in spending time with them when they

67

could spend the time together? He had smiled at that, enjoying her romantic logic despite having mild misgivings that it was not how things should progress given that he had every intention of marrying this beautiful, captivating, quixotic woman.

Arundhati emerged wearing tight jeans, decorated with lace and diamanté, sandals embossed with gold, and a t-shirt proudly announcing it to be a Versace which seemed highly unlikely. Her black hair was worn long and loose, arranged in waves around her shoulders and she smiled at him, her lips parting to show a perfect set of white teeth. He leaped out of the rickshaw to meet her, his hand reaching for hers to guide her inside. She peered up at him from underneath her hair, her large black kohl-rimmed eyes laughing flirtatiously.

"You are so old-fashioned, Prakash. Do you think I can't get into a taxi by myself?" and a peel of laughter drifted through the air as she lowered herself into her seat.

Prakash was never sure how to respond to her mocking. She teased him regularly, and when he questioned her hurtful comments, she laughed it off telling him not to take her seriously, after which she would usually give him a hug or a passionate kiss. He found her quite baffling and totally fascinating.

If they had been in Calicut, he would have taken her to his club of which he was inordinately proud. Being a member of a club was an honour, a sign of success. There was an exclusivity about being a member which pleased him; he was part of an elite sector of society – not yet the top level, but he had aspirations and ambition. But here in Ahmedabad, he didn't have that option so he had booked to have dinner at Vishalla, a restaurant he had been taken to on business that had impressed him as being someplace special. Nestled in grounds on the edge of the city, it offered more than just a meal at a table. It was designed to make the visitor feel that they had entered a village, offering entertainment, with gardens to explore and enjoy, a shop and even a museum. He glanced in her direction and tightened his lips. He wished she had dressed differently, much as he loved seeing her curves squeezed into those close-fitting jeans, he felt that they and the t-shirt had a casual appearance that was inappropriate for his plans tonight. There was nothing he could do about it now, though, as it would ruin the atmosphere between them if he mentioned his wish for her to change into something more classic.

He had planned it all out. They would go for a walk around the gardens, enjoying the surroundings, followed by dinner, during which he would ask her if she would like him to approach her parents and ask for her hand in marriage. He smiled at the thought and his stomach churned with excitement at the dream of having her to himself, for himself, to come home to at night, in his bed... He groaned audibly and then cleared his throat to cover the unexpected sound. Arundhati glanced at him and placed her hand on his thigh.

"What are you thinking, Prakash?"

He waggled his head and patted her hand, replacing it on her lap. He was not in a state to withstand any escalation of physical excitement and he needed a moment to get himself back under control. The sooner he asked her the better, and then he could move onto organising the wedding and then...

The taxi arrived and Prakash reminded the driver of their negotiations, making sure he would wait for them before leading her to the entrance, his stomach fluttering with unexpected nerves.

He guided her towards the garden, explaining that if they had been in his city, he would, of course, have taken her to his club, clarifying its exclusivity, describing what events happened there and looked at her for signs of awe. This was his moment to impress her and show her, if there was any doubt, that he was a good match. She asked questions about the members; what they did and who they were and he was satisfied. They strolled at a leisurely pace through the garden, stopping to watch the puppet show with figures performing various dances and even snake charming acts manipulated with great dexterity by puppeteers using strings looped over their fingers. They moved on to watch the folk dancing, and she clapped her hands at the woman balancing the tower of bowls on her head as she moved gracefully. Finally, Prakash heard his name called and he led her to the restaurant where they were seated on cushions on the hard mud floor. He was pleased, this place was magical and the perfect setting. He was pleased that everything had been carefully thought out. A waiter arrived with a jug of water for them to rinse their hands.

Prakash took a deep breath and then said, "Have you been here before?"

Arundhati shook her head. "No. But it's nice."

He smiled. "I'm glad you like it. I wanted to take you somewhere special. If we had been in Calicut, I would have taken you to my club," he repeated.

She smiled at him. "Yes, you told me already." She paused and then said, "I have never been to a club, but soon I expect to see many. I am going to travel the world and see everything I can. I plan to be in first class and meet loads of important people – who knows what might happen?" She raised an eyebrow and smiled broadly at him, her head tilted to one side.

Prakash felt his jaw drop. The speech he had so carefully planned had evaporated into the warm air that threatened to stifle him.

"I don't understand. How can you afford to travel the world in first class?" was all he managed to stammer.

Arundhati leaned towards him, animated and excited. "I am going to be a flight attendant. I will be very good at it, don't you think?" She thrust one shoulder forwards, peering over at him provocatively and then threw her head back with a throaty laugh.

He clasped his hands tightly together. "Have you been accepted with an airline?"

She nodded. "Of course. I told you, I'm a natural. I'm going to go far."

"What about marriage, children? You don't want to leave it too late. A career is all very well, but you want to know that you will be well looked after, in comfort, and have some stability in your life."

Arundhati stared at him. "Stability? Be looked after? How old do you think I am, 65? I'm 20, Prakash! I've got loads of time before I settle down – if I settle down at all. I want adventure and excitement. I want to see what's outside my city."

Prakash floundered in his state of shock. "Calicut has a lot to offer. Our spice market is one of the best in the world. There's my club – you don't get membership if you are just anyone. My home is in one of the best neighbourhoods in Calicut. We have a maid, a driver, and a cook." He lowered his voice, trying to gain control. "Maybe you just need to look closer to home to see what is on offer for you. You don't have to live in a flat and work in a shop."

Arundhati stared back at him. She paused, then said, "Are you proposing to me, Prakash? You think you can offer me the best? You will offer me boredom, living with your ma and pa, having babies and stuck at home while you work. No, Prakash, that's not for me. I don't need you to look after me, I can look after myself and I'm going to see what is out there in the world, outside of this boring city, and make the best choice when I see all my options. I'm going to make something of myself. I'm not going to be stuck in a backwater."

Prakash slumped, his dream shattered, his mind trying to grapple with what had just happened to his carefully laid out plan.

"I see."

The ornately dressed waiter arrived with the thali, placing the array of sumptuous dishes in front of them and stepping back with a bow. Arundhati reached in with her fingers, expressing delight at the taste.

"*Mmm*, Prakash, you must taste these sabjis, they are delicious. You like Gujarati food?"

"I prefer Keralan food. It is more delicate," he answered abruptly.

Suddenly, he realised he could hardly bear to look at Arundhati. They ate their meal in silence and after paying the bill, they walked back to the awaiting rickshaw and drove to her apartment block.

There had been no conversation between the two of them, nor had he leaped out to see her to her door. If she wanted her independence, she could have it.

He flew back the next morning and was glad to be home. Removing his shoes and socks, he enjoyed feeling the cool polished floor underneath his feet, calming his heated temper. He opened the living room door and found his mother seated on the sofa watching her favourite soap opera on the television. She looked at him with surprise, sensing that something had changed in his manner, and patted the empty space beside her.

"Ma, I think maybe it is a good idea to look at those

photographs, after all?"

His mother smiled and thanked Shiva for yis generosity. She would offer a blessing later, after making sure that she made the most of this moment, this window of opportunity. She didn't know what had happened, and she wasn't going to ask.

Chapter 11
Mumbai 2018

Ajay reclined on his sun lounger, his large body filling the aluminium frame. His body was firm rather than fleshy and was still powerful, showing a legacy of having once being strong and muscly, but now perhaps with the emphasis more on strong and less on the muscly. A domed stomach loomed above his swimming pants and he wore a short-sleeved shirt open at the front to reveal a thick golden chain. His chest was hairy, the dense darkness sprinkled with grey in contrast to the hair on his head which was well oiled and perfectly black. His arms were also covered in copious hair which had earned him the moniker, 'baalon vaala', 'the hairy one.' On the wrist of one hand, he wore a large gold watch. The other hand, the fingers of which were adorned with gold rings, some inlaid with jewels, was slowly revolving a glass of whisky. He exuded authority.

A few things were bothering him; things he couldn't explain and he didn't like things not to be explained. Arundhati was dead. That in itself was not exactly a surprise; after all, he had sent Mansingh to kill her, only for him to discover that someone had done the job already. That in itself was not a problem. She had served her purpose well and he could live without her. But he had been informed by his handler that the valuable package she had been carrying had been short by some diamonds. Mansingh had searched everywhere in Arundhati's hotel room, but had failed to find the missing jewels, so the unanswered questions were; who had killed Arundhati, how had he known about the diamonds and, most importantly, where were they? He growled at the thought that someone had dared mess with him. Didn't they know what he would do in retaliation? He let out a snort at the thought of the retribution that he would take. Nobody stole from Ajay and got away with it. Perhaps Jitu and Vasant would return with good news for him. It was about time for them to be back.

Ajay gulped back the whisky and a manservant came running to collect the glass from him. "Another drink, sir?"

He shook his head, waving the young man away and heaved himself off the lounger. It was time to cool off in the pool. He stepped into the water and immersed himself fully, enjoying the feeling of weightlessness before emerging for air, his lungs gasping for breath. Everything he did was worth it for this. His pool. His servants. His mansion. His empire. He had grown up in Mumbai and he had first-hand experience of what it was like to be without money. Living in the slums. Nobody was going to take anything away from him. The brief respite he had felt being submerged in the water now evaporated and his anger and annoyance at the theft returned. He swam to the edge of the infinity pool and heaved himself out.

Immediately, a manservant arrived with a fresh white towel and rubbed him down before presenting Ajay with a robe. He acquiesced and offered his arms to be placed into the sleeves and the belt to be tied around his powerful paunch.

Another servant appeared at the sliding glass doors that opened from the patio into the lounge and announced the arrival of Jitu and Vasant. Ajay walked towards the two men, one thin and one large like an Indian Laurel and Hardy and raised one eyebrow in expectation.

"Well? I hope you have some good news for me. Did you find anything in the flat?"

Jitu cleared his throat.

"Someone had already got to the flat, sir. We arrived, there was no one there, but everything was everywhere. It was a terrible mess."

Ajay roared with anger.

"This is impossible! Someone is one step ahead of us and I am not happy. Not happy at all. You saw no one?"

Jitu and Vasant exchanged looks.

Vasant answered, "There was a woman who came to the flat so we grabbed her thinking she might know something."

Ajay looked at them, and scanned the room ostentatiously. Spreading his arms wide, he said, "I don't see a woman! Where is she?"

Vasant grinned. "Ajay sir, it was very exciting. She was Detective Inspector McKinley. You know... on Netflix? She is English and was very nice. We were going to drop her off at her hotel but her driver was waiting. Imagine we nearly had her in our car. It was very unexpected."

Ajay looked at them both, his eyes moving from one thin face with chiselled cheekbones to the other man, his rounder, more thickset features beaming with pleasure.

"You are telling me that you pulled a woman, an actress, into your car and then let her go?"

Jitu nodded. "Yes, sir. She is famous. You must be knowing Detective Inspector McKinley? She is half-Indian," he added.

"She could be half camel for all I care! What was she doing at the flat?"

"She told us she had met the owner on her holiday only... in Goa...and was just visiting him at his Mumbai apartment to say

76

hello. I am so happy that we hadn't hurt her before we knew that."

Ajay stared at them, and decided it wasn't worth punching them just yet for their utter stupidity. He would follow this lead – the only lead he had so far – with a more subtle manoeuvre.

Pulling out his phone, he scrolled down to M and pressed the number. "Mansingh?"

A rich deep voice answered, "Ajaybhai, I have everyone with eyes and ears open for news of any action taken against you, but nothing yet. No one has been boasting about killing your woman or taking your goods. I am so sorry. I will sort this out, Ajay, even if it kills me, I promise."

"Mansingh, I trust you more than anyone I know. Why else would I send you to put an end to that woman bothering me? She was threatening me with exposing my life, the business I have worked hard on and set up from nothing. You understand what that means to me. Who else would I trust to collect the goods that she was trying to steal from me?"

"You do me a great honour, Ajaybhai. I am only sorry that I was unable to do what you asked. If only I had arrived a little sooner."

Ajay ran his fingers through his hair.

"I want you to do something for me. There's an actress here from England, perhaps on holiday, perhaps linked to the missing package. I don't know. She went to the flat in Mumbai that belongs to that 'friend' of Arundhati. I want you to find out what she knows. Get a bit friendly with her." He chuckled. "You see? I only give you nice jobs." He continued, "I don't know where she is staying, but I am sure it will be no problem for you to find her. Her name is…" He looked towards Vasant who answered, "McKinley."

Jitu elbowed him hard. "Sorry, sir, that's her film name. Her real name is…" and his voice trailed off nervously. He looked to Jitu for help who shrugged in response.

Ajay rolled his eyes. "These idiots don't know her real name, but her film name is Detective Inspector McKinley."

"Detective Inspector McKinley! *Acha*, her real name is Indy Monroe. Boss, I love that programme." He paused. "She's very famous. I can see why you don't want to get heavy with her, it would be bad publicity."

Jitu and Vasant wobbled their heads, exchanging broad, smug smiles.

"Don't worry, Ajay, I'll find out where she is and what she knows and get back to you as soon as possible."

Ajay clicked off and stared at the two men in front of him. "Get out of my sight," He growled. Watching them go, he sat down heavily in his armchair and crossed his ankle over the opposite knee, his foot wiggling up and down rapidly as he mused on the turn of events.

Mansingh had known of this woman too…hmmm… he was a Bollywood man himself through and through. In fact, Bollywood was a lucrative business for him. He turned his mind to this unknown actress. The chances were that she was just on holiday in the wrong place at the wrong time. Still, it was best to be sure.

He opened up his computer and googled her name. There she was – several times over. The lead in a Netflix series that had been running for six years, broadcast worldwide.

Married an actor on the series then divorced him in a high-profile tabloid scandal due to him having an affair with one of the extras. There was a question mark over whether the series was going to continue. He scanned the publicity photos of her; dressed up on the red carpet, at home with her husband, as

Detective Inspector McKinley... there were no shortage of images. She was pretty, he thought, but too skinny for his taste. He preferred proper curves, the sort of curves you found on women like Priyanka Chopra... breasts, buttocks, thighs, big eyes, large lips, the lot. He liked to handle a woman, to grab her and hold her. What was this fashion for skin and bones? A woman like that could slip through your arms and you would hardly know you'd ever had her. His thoughts turned to Arundhati. He chuckled. Now she was worth having. He sat back in his chair and pondered. If Indy Monroe hadn't ransacked the apartment, who had? And where were his diamonds...

Chapter 12
Mumbai 2015

Arundhati brushed her lipstick carefully within the pencilled outline she had drawn round her lips and then pressed them firmly into a tissue. She repeated the process and sighed. This was a long haul flight and she had to look perfect for the passengers. She parted her lips and bared her teeth, making sure that there were no lipstick stains, then double-checked the rest of her makeup. She had applied full foundation, some contouring to highlight her cheekbones, then had enhanced her large deep-set eyes with eyeshadow that accentuated the depth of her eyelids, highlighting the lids themselves. She dusted it off to set and then framed the lot with a bold line of black liquid eyeliner, followed by lashings of mascara. She gazed at her image in the full-length mirror. Smoothing her tightly fitting burgundy skirt over her curvaceous hips, she turned from side to side to ensure that it hugged her curves as much as the pre-flight inspection would allow, then buttoned her jacket. Arundhati had swept her hair into a tight bun that was secured firmly into place with the aid of a matching scrunchy and copious hairpins and hairspray – there was no tolerance for casual dishevelled hairstyles for the cabin crew of Qatar Airways – and the final cherry on top was the scarlet pillbox hat. She was ready to go.

It had been four years since she had begun her career as an air stewardess and the novelty and excitement of the job had palled slightly. She had been thrilled to travel to new, unknown countries and excited to stay in hotels courtesy of the airlines, enjoying the exploration of the tastes, smells and sights of the world. This job had given her freedom and independence, and had introduced her to different cultures and a much better lifestyle. It was a pleasure being part of a team, making friends with the other members of the crew who had become her family in this adventure. Arundhati had worked hard to be promoted from economy to business class and had started her training, which was extensive and rigorous, to be a first class flight attendant. She had been surprised to find that the passengers in business class were often more demanding than in economy, but there were fewer of them to deal with and, so far as she was concerned, they were a much better class of people. She appreciated the higher standards of business class, as well as the more comfortable conditions. Many of the travellers on business and first class flights were regulars and she took pride in the mutual recognition and personal service she would offer them. Arundhati was ambitious and aware that she was in her prime and needed to make the most of her opportunities. She would complete her first class training and enjoy a couple of years at the top. But then what? This was her chance to meet the crème de la crème of people, people who could afford to spend thousands on one flight and she wasn't going to waste it. She would take advantage of the opportunities available.

The cabin crew for the flight from Cape Town to Mumbai gathered in the lobby of the hotel before boarding the bus that took them to their terminal. There had been no parties the night before. It had been a short stopover for them and this was going to be a long haul with a stopover in Doha. The sort of stopover that was neither long enough to give the crew a decent break, or short enough to keep the adrenaline going. Being a flight attendant on Qatar Airlines was hard work – harder work than Arundhati had envisaged. It took a lot of energy to be consistently good natured, maintaining a smiling facade while being instantly helpful for hours on end, anticipating any problems that might occur, and able to deal with medical and/or personality issues with calmness and efficiency. She had learned to value her hotel room isolation and downtime.

Arundhati was pleased Priya was also going to be in business class with her today. Working with crew you liked and trusted made so much difference on a flight.

The bus arrived at the terminal and the crew moved like clockwork along the familiar route through security to their gate. They knew the airports backwards; where their favourite coffee was, which shops were where, how long it took to get from A to B. Most of the airport staff were familiar too and they breezed through security with smiling acknowledgement that they were all in this together – the smooth running of international travel in its own strangely isolated and complete world.

After gaining the necessary approval for their appearance and uniform, Arundhati and Priya entered the plane, trundling their hand luggage suitcases next to them.

They stored their belongings away, and then, removing their jackets and hats and replacing heels with more comfortable flat shoes, like a well-oiled machine, they prepared the cabin for entry. Everything had to be perfect.

The passengers were welcomed by the smiling crew, helped with their hand luggage and when they were settled, offered glasses of champagne and warm towels. Priya and Arundhati had checked the passenger names on the list to see if there were any passengers with special requirements, or names of people they knew before choosing which side of the cabin they were going to work on. There was one name Arundhati recognised as being somebody she had attended to on a previous flight and she treated him to an especially warm smile as she offered him his drink. Not champagne, but whisky, Glenfiddich, with a small jug of water on the side.

Ajay looked up at her as she leaned over him with the tray. His eyes scanned her breasts, her body covered discreetly in a tight-fitting camisole beneath the thin blouse, before reaching her face and noticing the full lips and the perfectly white teeth.

"You remembered." He arched a thick black eyebrow and removed the glass from the tray, raising it to her to indicate a toast of appreciation.

Arundhati smiled. "If there's anything you need during the flight, please let me know, sir."

"Ajay," he answered.

She tilted her head to one side in acknowledgement of the invitation. "I hope you enjoy your flight," she responded carefully.

She stood up and turned, aware of his gaze. She would attend to him carefully, she thought, smiling to herself.

The flight was fully booked. Cape Town to Doha was a ten-hour flight and this was daytime, so the passengers would not be readying themselves for a night's sleep, but expecting breakfast and lunch with snacks and drinks throughout.

Arundhati and Priya worked the thirty-six seats with efficiency, responding to the individual requests for the a la carte menu choices, organising and preparing the food and drinks, and attending to the needs of the customers. They were glad of the moments when they found themselves together behind the scenes and away from the public eye.

"So, what's going on with the man in seat 4A?" Priya asked as she placed the bottle of Sauvignon Blanc on the tray alongside the smoked salmon hors d'oeuvre.

"Nothing, he's just flirting. You know what these men can be like," Arundhati answered. Much as she liked Priya, it seemed best to be circumspect. She did not want to invite gossip about her behaviour. It was best to be careful.

Priya glanced over at her. "I thought you were seeing Prakash?" Arundhati turned to look at her. Priya sighed and rolled her eyes. "What. You've broken up with him?" She waited for a response.

"His wife is pregnant," Arundhati answered.

Priya's jaw dropped. "Really! *Meri dost*, it's time to finish this affair, no?"

Arundhati nodded in reply and then peered towards her friend cheekily. "Maybe." She laughed.

She turned her head in the direction of the man who exuded power and charisma and… She turned back to look at her friend, grinning. "What do you know about 4A?"

Priya returned the look, her eyes narrowing. "He's a big businessman, in property I think. Flies with us regularly. Be careful, Arundhati… let's say, I wouldn't want to get on the wrong side of him."

She wobbled her head thoughtfully. "Don't worry, I am attending to him only, Priya. Being the best flight attendant Qatar requires." She laughed.

Priya smiled. "Attend to him, but don't give him extra attention – you think I don't notice? Take care, Arundhati." She reached her hand towards her friend affectionately, then picked up her tray.

"Back to work, eh?" She smiled, heading into the cabin.

Chapter 13
Mumbai 2018

The man glanced up from his cup of coffee and caught the eye of the attractive woman who could almost be Indian. She looked away quickly before slowly turning to look at him. She had noticed him before. It seemed they were both morning coffee regulars at 15 Cafe. She had to admit she liked the look of him. Tall with thick black hair, clean shaven, neatly dressed in a hand block printed shirt and jeans. She liked the fact that he arrived each morning with a book. Not many men read in her experience. It demonstrated culture and an ability to focus; qualities rare these days.

She turned back to her coffee and sighed. It was time to move on from Mumbai, she thought. It had been two days since her terrifying experience in Prakash's flat. Indy had rerun the incident over and over in her mind, trying to make sense of it. They had asked her what she had been doing in Prakash's flat and they were looking for something – what?

Prakash had been very lucky that he had gone home to Sonal and not to his flat in Mumbai. Had he known they were coming? What on earth was going on? She shook her head in response to her thoughts. It was no longer her business. Sonal was happy to have Prakash back and she was released from her promise to Sonal now. She was on holiday and all she should be thinking about was her next destination.

"Excuse me."

Indy turned in response to the warm voice that had interrupted her musings and saw the man in the beautiful shirt standing respectfully by her side.

"I hope you don't mind me approaching you, but I wondered if you have seen the famous sights here in Mumbai?"

She frowned and turned away. So he was just another local touting for business. What a shame.

"I don't need a guide, thank you, and I would like to be on my own." Her voice was hard and dismissive and she waited for him to move away, but was experienced enough to know that it might not be that easy. It seemed Indians did not take no for an answer when they were trying to sell you something. She was surprised to be accosted like this here in this cafe though. She had enjoyed the peace of 15 Cafe and had felt relaxed and safe from the hassle of people vying for her attention, offering her a myriad of purchases everywhere she went.

He laughed. "I am not a guide. I'm here as a tourist and am on my own. I wondered if you had any advice for me as to what is the best thing to see here in Mumbai." The man looked at her. His expression was that of amusement and she blushed in embarrassment.

"Oh, I am so sorry!" Indy gestured to the seat next to her. "Won't you join me? I thought you were…" She hesitated, aware that she was in imminent danger of sounding racist and offensive.

"You thought I was trying to sell you something?" he chuckled. "It's OK. It's my fault for not introducing myself properly." He held out his hand. "Mansingh. On my own and on holiday and seeing the sights of our beautiful country." He smiled. "Yes, we have many people trying to earn a living in whatever way they can. Selling directly is often the easiest option. There is no salesman as good as the one who needs to put food on the table for his family."

Indira blushed again.

"No problem, it can be annoying to me too." He laughed.

He had eased the tension and she lifted her eyes to look at him gratefully.

He continued, "So, do you have any recommendations?"

He placed a guide to Mumbai on the table and flicked through the highlights with his finger, asking her what was worth seeing and she felt pleased to be able to offer him her opinion, telling him what needed to be booked in advance, what could be crossed off his list, and together they devised a schedule.

"Do you have plans today or shall we start straight away?" he asked.

The cultural differences between India and the UK never ceased to surprise her. It would have taken weeks back home before someone she had just met in a coffee shop presumed that she would be joining him, let alone asking her if she wanted to go right now. Throwing caution to the winds, she embraced the invitation with delight.

"I have no plans at all." She grinned. "Would you like me to be your guide? Let the adventure begin."

Indy and Mansingh entered the Taj Hotel hot and sticky, despite the welcome breeze from the boat trip that had carried them from the Elephanta Caves to the perfect location for afternoon tea in sumptuous surroundings. They both made their excuses to visit the restrooms to tidy up and arranged to meet again at the Sea Lounge refreshed and ready to enjoy a very British afternoon tea.

The Sea Lounge was painted a restful cool aquamarine, the arches within the very large room creating a feeling of both space and privacy. It was a wonderful merging of east and west in architecture and interior decor. The tiered plate of sandwiches and cakes arrived with a pot of tea and Indy grinned, tucking into it with relish. She loved travelling, but it was moments like this that made her really nostalgic for home, even if it was a colonial concept of the British abroad. Was there anything more British than afternoon tea? She chuckled to herself.

"Have you been here before?" she asked Mansingh.

He smiled and shook his head. "It would not even cross my mind to come into the Taj. It is the most expensive hotel in India, I think."

Indy paused, mentally kicking herself at her thoughtlessness. Of course. This would be beyond the reach of most Indians; how could she have asked such an ignorant question? She made a mental note to make this her treat.

"Excuse me." She turned to see a young woman with long dark hair who stood with a broad smile to her side, a phone in her hand. "You are Detective Inspector McKinley? Could I have a photo with you?" She handed the mobile to Mansingh and leaned down, her hands resting on each of Indy's shoulders, her face instantly forming an automatic picture perfect smile. Mansingh returned the phone.

"You took more than one?" she asked him, then accepting his head bobble, she thanked Indy and spun round on her heels back to her table.

Indy looked at him, gauging his reaction. "Does that happen often?" he asked.

She tilted her head to one side and then nodded reluctantly. "Yes, quite often."

"So you are a famous policewoman?" He furrowed his brow to convey his confusion as to why a member of the public should be interested in being photographed with her.

Indy laughed. "No, I'm an actor who plays Detective Inspector McKinley in a series." She paused, waiting to see if the name resonated with him at all, and was pleased that there was no reaction. "You don't watch Netflix?"

He shook his head. "Not much. I prefer to read. But maybe I will now. What is the series called?"

Her hand clasped the handle of the teapot as she poured herself another cup of tea, offering him one, before answering lightly, "D I McKinley," then laughing raucously.

A delighted smile spread across his face. "So I am with a celebrity then."

She shrugged. "And you? You haven't told me what you do."

"My work is probably not that interesting to you. It's certainly not as exciting as being an actress in a series. I work at NID, the National Institute of Design; a college in Ahmedabad, Gujarat."

He could see a look of recognition in her eyes. "You have heard of it?" he said with some surprise. The college was one of the best in the country but he had not expected her to know that.

She shook her head. "No. But I have heard of Ahmedabad. My mother's family comes from there." She hesitated and then continued, "My mother is Gujarati and my father Scottish. My full name is Indira Monroe. They met on a train during his gap year." Noticing Mansingh's eyebrows furrow, she explained, "It's quite usual to take a year between the final year of school and starting college or university, and a lot of people use the time to travel and see something of the world."

He raised his eyebrows. "How fortunate people in the west are to be able to afford to do that. In India, we have to be super competitive. There are over a billion people fighting for the best jobs. To take a year off to 'see the world' would be a luxury that most people could not afford."

Indy bit her lip. "It's not that my dad was ever well off," she attempted to explain, then shrugged her shoulders. "Anyway, he was on the train in Gujarat and met my mother. I think it was love at first sight. But my mother's family had other ideas for her. They were not impressed by him. He looked like a bum – this was the 70s; he had long hair, a beard, hippy clothes, no job and was and still is a fervent atheist. There was nothing about him that made him husband material for their beloved daughter. My mum and dad kept in touch, writing letters – the idea of letters seems so romantic to me now – and when he finished his college course, he got a job. He started as a carpenter and went into furniture making. He sent her a plane ticket, she arrived in Scotland and they got married. Her parents never forgave her and I have never met them. I wasn't brought up speaking Gujarati which I realise is a shame now, but when I was a child, I was desperate to fit in. I come from a small town and multicultural marriages were rare – still are, really. With a name like Indira, and looking slightly 'exotic', I was sometimes the focus of unwanted attention, shall we say." She grimaced. "I gave up trying to get people to say 'Indira' with the accent on the 'In', not the 'dir', and insisted on being called Indy. It's worked to a certain extent; my new name doesn't draw attention to my ethnicity.' She raised her eyes to his and laughed. "Sorry, I didn't mean to bore you with my life story."

Mansingh smiled. "Please don't apologise. It is very interesting to me."

"There's another connection with Ahmedabad…" she said thoughtfully. "Someone who came from there died recently." She faltered, unsure of what to share with him.

He leaned forward, "Someone important?" he asked gently.

She looked at him, shaking her head vigorously. "Oh no, nothing like that. Not family or anything." She saw his look of sympathy and plowed on quickly. "I never met her. You see…" She paused again, wondering if it were wise to continue. She had only just met this man. But then, she reasoned, why shouldn't she share her strange story.

His gaze was gentle and inviting as she began, telling him about her meeting with Sonal and Prakash, Sonal confiding in her husband's possible affair with Arundhati. She paused.

Somehow, her trip to Antwerp seemed crazy, so she omitted it and skipped forwards to visiting Prakash in Mumbai and finding his flat ransacked by two scary men before being released thanks to the fame of Detective Inspector McKinley.

Mansingh took her hand. "That must have been terrifying for you." His voice expressed shock.

Indy squeezed his hand. "It was. For a moment, I thought I was going to be killed – or worse." She shuddered. It was a relief to talk about it with someone, she realised. Up until now, she had kept this experience to herself, holding all that tension within her. She felt her body relax gratefully.

"And Sonal? What does she think now?"

Indy looked at him. "She seems fine. Prakash is home and the woman he was maybe having an affair with is… no longer a worry." She hesitated a moment.

"But?" Mansingh probed.

Indy looked at him with a puzzled expression on her face. "I don't know. It's silly really, but it's just that Sonal lied to me about being home when I know she wasn't, and for the life of me I can't think why she would do that. I don't know, maybe she bought an expensive dress and didn't want to tell me." She laughed, then furrowed her brow. "I have no idea who those men were and I don't know what they were looking for, but quite frankly," she said, shaking her head and inhaling deeply, "it's none of my business any more."

He looked at her. "You are not even curious?"

She grinned. "Well, yes, a bit. But there's not much I can do about it really. I think it's time to move on and start my holiday over again. There's so much of India I haven't seen."

He paused. "This might sound a little forward, but I have had a lovely day and have really enjoyed being with you. If you want to come to Ahmedabad – for any reason – I would be delighted to show you around my city. I could return the favour and be your tour guide." He smiled.

She returned his smile. "I would love that. I was wondering where to go next after Mumbai, and it's always nice to know someone in a city." She hesitated. "But don't worry about having to look after me, I'm very independent and don't want to cause you any trouble."

"No problem at all. It will be a great honour to show you Ahmedabad." He put his palms together and bowed his head.

"Wonderful" – she smiled – "and to thank you for your generous invitation, this tea is my treat."

Her trip to India was definitely looking up.

Chapter 14
Calicut 2013

Prakash rolled over in bed and kissed his wife on the cheek. She reached her arm around him and snuggled into his body.

"I have to go to work, Sonal."

"Noooo," she moaned. "Stay here for a little longer, why don't you?" She moved her arm down underneath his cotton pyjama bottoms, stroking him between his legs. He groaned, feeling his penis harden. Sonal chuckled. "See? Your body wants to stay."

Prakash moved his body away from her caressing hand and rolled out of bed. His wife was not going to control him, manipulating him to stay in bed when he had told her clearly he needed to get to work.

"I'm sorry, Sonal, but I have deliveries to look after. When I say I have to go to work, I mean it."

Sonal frowned. "I'm so bored, Prakash. You go to work every day and what can I do? I just wait for you to come back."

He closed his eyes and sighed. Why couldn't she manage to find something that interested her and kept her busy? He was tired of repeatedly making the same suggestions to her – get a hobby, meet up with friends, get a part-time job, do a cookery course…

"Perhaps you and my mother could go out somewhere…?" his voice trailed off as Sonal's dark eyes glared at him.

"You know your mother isn't interested in doing anything

with me. She either sits in this house watching television or goes out with her friends."

"Well, you could—"

"Don't tell me I could go with her. Why would I want to spend time with her friends? They are much older than me." Sonal pouted, then whined, "I wish you would spend more time with me. I miss you, Prakash."

He walked over to her and sat beside her on the bed.

"I need to go to work, Sonal. But I'll be back for dinner tonight. You need to find something to keep you occupied. Go to classes and learn something new and maybe make some friends." He kissed her lightly and stood up. He needed a shower, but most of all he needed to get away from this endless conversation that never went anywhere.

Sonal rolled over, pulling the sheet over her head. She hated living with his parents. He was too close to his mother and she constantly felt undermined by her. It was Prakash's mother who decided what meals they would eat, who told the servants what to do, who was there making sure Prakash had his breakfast on time, who got the cook to prepare his tiffin. Sonal had given up making suggestions and trying to find a role for herself in the household, let alone the marriage. The only time she ever felt she had Prakash's full attention was when they were in bed. At least his mother couldn't join them there.

There was a knock on the door.

"Prakash?" It was his mother. "Your breakfast is waiting for you. You are a little late today," she added.

Sonal snarled under the light cotton sheet and mimicked his mother's words, mocking her voice. She threw aside the cover and grabbed her light cotton robe. Opening the door to their bathroom, she saw Prakash was shaving and leaned against the doorframe, one hand on her hip.

"Your mother says you're late for breakfast."

"Tell her I'll be down shortly," he answered.

Sonal raised her eyes to the ceiling and closed the bathroom door behind her as she left the bedroom and headed down to the kitchen and Prakash's mother.

Calicut wholesale spice market on Big Bazaar Rd was a vibrant scene. Lorries with brightly painted designs, laden with sacks of spices blocked the streets as bullocks hauling carts vied for space while bicycles and rickshaws weaved between them. Load carrying men shifted their sacks back and forth, their mundus wrapped around their waist, the hems tucked up to skirt length for ease. Dust filled the air, there was an incessant honking of horns as drivers negotiated the bustling streets and the smells of spices, dirt and excrement pervaded the senses. This was not a tourist area. This was a working street with its focus on business. Prakash's shop was halfway down Big Bazaar Rd. Like most other shops, the frontage was open, revealing the huge open sacks filled with various spices, chillies, cumin seeds, cinnamon sticks, garam masala, black pepper, cardamom pods and much much more.

Prakash signed off deliveries as he directed the supervisor, who directed the men, offloading, arranging, sweeping. Inside was a hive of activity to match the bustle of the street outside.

His phone rang and removing it from his pocket, he saw with surprise that Arundhati's name appeared on the screen. Prakash hesitated, recognising the danger of reigniting their relationship, at the same time as he realised his thumb had pressed the accept button. "Prakash!" he heard and his stomach flipped at the sound of her voice.

"Arundhati." What else was there to say?

"Prakash, I am in Calicut for one night only. Do you want to meet me? It would be so lovely to see you again after such a long time. You are married, *yar*?" She chuckled. "So, I wasn't your one and only love then?" Prakash heard a peel of laughter. "Just joking. So... dinner? Eight p.m.?"

Prakash heard his voice answer, "We could go to Paragon?"

"No, Prakash, the queues are too long at Paragon. Let's go to Salkaram on the beach, yes? Nice views and a little quieter. See you there at eight p.m. You remember what I look like, yes?" Another peel of laughter and the phone clicked dead.

Prakash stared at the rectangular object in his hand. Just like that, it had brought Arundhati back into his life when she should not be there. He would meet her this one night only, ask her how she was and put her out of his life again.

The rest of the day continued with Prakash on auto-pilot. If anyone had asked him which order had just been delivered, he would have had to refer to his paperwork to answer. His mind revolved around his conversation with Arundhati, the sound of her voice and her throaty laughter. Why had she called him? Was it just to catch up, a reunion of old friends, or was it something more...?

Six p.m. came and Prakash arrived home dusty and on edge. He kicked off his sandals and entered the hall. Sonal appeared almost immediately, her face expressing relief, her timing indicating that she had been waiting for him to arrive at any moment. He clenched his jaw fighting back the guilt and leaned towards her, giving her a light kiss on the cheek.

"I am sorry, Sonal, I am very dirty. It was so hot today and there were a lot of deliveries. I will go upstairs and take a shower." He paused, wondering if there was a better way of saying it, but nothing sprung to mind. "I have to go out tonight. It's a business meeting, and I won't be back for dinner." He avoided her gaze as he turned to go up the stairs.

"What business meeting? And so sudden? You never mentioned it this morning. Does Ma know?"

Prakash ran up the stairs. "Business is business, Sonal. It's what pays for your dresses."

Sonal frowned and walked across the large hall towards the living room door.

"Ma? Did you know Prakash is not home for dinner tonight?"

His mother reluctantly peeled her eyes from the television set and turned towards Sonal. "Not in tonight? Where is he going?" Her eyes were wide.

Sonal shrugged. At least Ma hadn't known about this either.

"He says he has a business meeting." She turned to leave the room, crossed the hall and climbed the stairs. Her loneliness was tangible.

Pushing open their bedroom door, she sank onto the bed, aware that whatever she said was going to irritate him, but unable not to voice how she felt. Why couldn't he take her with him? Even a business meeting was better than another evening at home with only his mother to talk to.

Prakash emerged from the bathroom, his towel wrapped around his waist and clenched his teeth at the sight of her. He wanted to choose his outfit with Arundhati in mind and not with his wife watching.

He glanced over to her and saw to his surprise that she was smiling at him. Disconcerted, he managed a slight smile in response and felt his breath ease and the tension in his body relax. Sonal patted the bed next to her and he moved towards her reluctantly. He didn't want to interact with his wife just now, he needed space to clear his head and gather his thoughts before meeting with Arundhati.

"Come, Prakash." Sonal stretched out her hand and stroked his face. "My handsome husband." She smiled. "Who is this businessman stealing you away from me tonight?"

Prakash pulled away slightly and cleared his throat. "No one you know, Sonal. It's just business. You know I would much rather be putting my feet up at home than going out tonight." He smiled nervously.

Sonal leaned forwards and stroked down his arm. "Perhaps I could come with you? I would love to go out and I could keep you company. Maybe I could be an asset?" She chuckled lightly.

Prakash blanched at the thought and felt totally tongue-tied.

"I wish you could, Sonal, but not tonight. It just wouldn't be right and these meetings are very boring. I will make it up to you. We will go out on Saturday." He looked at her. "Just the two of us," he said, leaning over and kissing her on the lips. She clasped her arms around him and held him to her so tightly that he had to extricate himself gently from her hold. "Saturday," he repeated, moving away.

She sighed, swung her legs to the floor and slammed the bedroom door.

Prakash squeezed his eyes closed and put his head in his hands. What was he doing? This was utter madness. Utter, utter madness.

Chapter 15
Goa 2015

The warm breeze drifted across the white sand and Arundhati laughed as she dug her toes into it, feeling the sand moulding under and around her feet as she buried them into the tiny particles. She observed the beautiful contrast of colour between her brown skin and the cream-coloured sand. This was a world away from growing up in Ahmedabad. Goa had a relaxed, liberated feeling; it was a place of pleasure and hedonism where she could enjoy walking down the beach in shorts and a crop top, and as she had never had the occasion to learn to swim, she was quite happy to splash in the water. In any case, she wouldn't dream of walking on the beach wearing a swimsuit or bikini, something that would undoubtedly have attracted unwanted attention from Indian men. It was one thing for westerners to go about half naked, but quite another for Indian women to expose themselves. Indian men could frolic in the sea wearing only their underpants, but women needed to be more careful.

Arundhati's swimsuit was saved for more private surroundings, like by the pool at Ajay's villa. She turned to Ajay and laughed with delight, her face a picture of happiness.

"Race you to the sea?" she challenged.

Ajay shook his head. He was dressed in clean, freshly ironed white cotton shorts and he did not intend to get them wet before lunch. He smiled at her, enjoying the innocence of her appreciation of a simple thing like sand and sea on a beach.

"I will watch you run to the sea," he said, "I enjoy watching you."

She tilted her head and pursed her lips together in a seductive smile, her hands stroking his freshly pressed shirt. "I like you watching me." And she spun around, racing across the sand and into the water, her long hair falling in perfectly formed waves around her back and shoulders, her peals of laughter drifting back to him as she skipped across the rippling waves.

They crossed back along the beach through the shade of the trees inland towards Zeebop by the Sea, an upmarket outdoor restaurant set back from the beach that specialised in freshly caught seafood. Ajay signalled authoritatively to the head waiter who arrived swiftly and guided them to their table and took their order.

He surveyed the area, appreciating the seclusion. The restaurant was like a well-known secret, off the beaten track, through the woods, small and exclusive. The waiters arrived at the tables with huge, freshly caught platters of seafood – fish, crab and lobster. Once chosen, and while the food was being cooked, there was time to swim or relax swinging in the hammocks in the shade of the trees. It was peaceful and felt secure.

"You like it here?" he asked Arundhati.

Arundhati nodded, smiling with delight.

Ajay looked at her. "So, you are enjoying Goa?"

"I love it, Ajay. Your home is beautiful and this is a perfect way to spend my time off. It's a real holiday." She leaned a bit closer towards him. "And, of course, I love being with you."

He nodded, satisfied. "Good."

Later that evening, Arundhati sat outside Ajay's villa,

overlooking the garden. There was a heady scent of jasmine in the warm air and she breathed it in, feeling it caress her body. She was wearing a long figure-hugging dress with a side split that allowed her to stretch out her leg, revealing smooth, shapely limbs adorned with a matching set of silver ankle bracelets, a gift from Ajay. She leaned back in her lounger and sighed. This was indeed the life that she had wanted and was now within her reach.

"A drink?" Ajay's deep voice interrupted her reverie.

Arundhati turned to look up at him. He had approached from behind her seat, coming from the direction of the house and when she nodded, he clicked his fingers and a boy came running. He ordered drinks for them both and reclined in the adjacent lounger.

"You look very beautiful tonight," he remarked.

She smiled. She felt beautiful tonight. Everything was perfect. "Arundhati, there is something I want you to do for me."

Her eyes turned to look at him inquisitively, trying to guess what was in his mind. It seemed to her that she had allowed him to do just about everything to her, an experience that, she had to admit, she had thoroughly enjoyed.

"I have some small items that I need to transport from one country to the other under the radar so to speak." Ajay watched her, gauging her response. This moment was key to their future – and hers. Her expression remained neutral, showing no signs of shock.

"For business purposes, I do not want to have to go through the bureaucracy of paperwork that would be necessary if I declared these items, so I thought it would be no problem for you to wear them for me."

Arundhati's eyes opened wide with surprise. "Wear them? What are they?"

Ajay's eyes gleamed. "Diamonds. You would wear them in

specially designed bras that look like flashy underwear. Nobody would believe you were wearing real jewels, worth thousands of dollars. All you have to do is to walk through security, and believe me, nothing will show up. With your job, it's perfect." He looked at her intensely, then smiled, his voice like rough velvet. "What do you say?"

She settled back in her chair and closed her eyes. "But of course, Ajay. No problem."

"You understand that this is never to be mentioned outside of my home?" The harsh edge to his voice was unmistakable.

Arundhati laughed nervously.

"This is no laughing matter, my dear. I demand complete loyalty and I will reward you well in return. However, betray me at cost to your life... or worse."

Arundhati felt a shiver run through her body, but at the same time she experienced a thrilling sensation at what was ahead of her.

This was her ticket to luxury, and all tickets have a price.

Chapter 16
Mumbai 2018

Prakash sat on the floor amidst the piles of upturned drawers and boxes, the contents of which were strewn around the flat. Personal letters were scattered across the floor, photographs of him with Arundhati that he had never been able to share with anyone apart from her were now displayed openly to strangers, and his stomach churned at the sight. This was his secret life, his private world, ripped open, handled, surveyed and thrown to the ground for all to see. Tears welled at the humiliation of this act and anger grew at the violation. Why would anyone do this to him?

A wave of fear ran through him and he jumped to his feet and ran to his bedside cabinet.

The drawer had been flung to the ground, the contents dispersed on the floor and he threw himself onto his knees, his hands wildly searching amongst the strewn items, for sight or feel of the last connection with Arundhati, but there was no sign of the packet that Arundhati had sent him. He crumpled at the realisation that the last connection with her had gone. She had sent him the packet by post before she went to Antwerp and he had opened it eagerly, bewildered to discover that inside was the locket he had given her some time ago, along with a note that asked him to keep it safe for her. He had no idea why she had done this, but hoped that it was because it meant something special to her because she loved him. He had placed it carefully inside the drawer beside his bed until they could be together again. Now it was gone and he would never see Arundhati again. His thoughts turned to the last time he had seen her and he shuddered at the memory of that afternoon.

Who had done this – and why?

He needed to eradicate all links between him and Arundhati. The letters, the photographs – everything. But first, he needed to rest. Crawling onto his bed, Prakash curled up into a tight little ball and closed his eyes tightly. He would get rid of the evidence tomorrow, before he went to breakfast and before he went home to Sonal.

Prakash sat at a table in one of his favourite places to eat, Cafe Mysore, a no-frills place that served fabulous South-Indian food. People could say what they want about foreign food but nothing replaced a great dosa, uttapam or idli with sambhar and chutneys. He was amazed to find when he travelled abroad, Keralan food was so hard to find. People would try to please him by taking him to Indian restaurants when he travelled, but the food was invariably North Indian, serving heavy curries, rice and breads. Where was the creamy coconut, the piles of nutty rice, the delicate dosa filled with masala, the fish curries or the flower-shaped appam? His mouth watered at the thought and he shook his head. Foreigners were so ignorant of his culture.

His breakfast arrived swiftly, a platter of vada rasam, hot idlis, pesarattu dosa and filter coffee. What made Cafe Madras so good was that the food was simple, freshly made and came quickly. He drew in a deep breath, inhaling the flavours before tucking in with his fingers enthusiastically. Truly, there was nothing as delicious as this.

He had slept surprisingly well and had woken up almost

expecting the ransacked flat to be a bad dream. Groaning at the sight of his scattered belongings, he had raised himself to his feet, bin bag in hand to gather up evidence of his private and personal connection to Arundhati and get rid of it. It was sad, but under the circumstances, essential. There must be no sign of their relationship. There wasn't much to collect and when he had finished, it had made little dent to the devastation around him. Sighed, he shook his head. He couldn't face dealing with it now. He had reached for his phone and called Sonal, telling her that he was coming home later today.

Prakash wiped his dish clean and headed to the hand wash to clean his fingers. Returning to his table, he saw two men; one large and round, the other skinny, sitting on the chairs opposite his seat. There was something about the pair that made him uneasy, but it was a busy restaurant and not unusual to share tables, he told himself as he approached nervously.

"You enjoyed your food?" the large one asked. The other man's bony face broke into a grin that revealed teeth that had seen better days. A ripple of unease travelled through his body as he picked up the bill and bobbled his head in response.

"You didn't leave anything for us," the man continued.

Prakash stared at him with uneasy surprise. "Do I know you?" he asked, twisting the piece of paper between his fingers nervously. His eyes scanned the busy cafe, the waiters carrying plates of food and empty dishes with focussed efficiency, the diners intent on filling their stomachs. He was invisible in a crowded room.

"No fuss, no worry, just keep calm," the big man said. "Hadn't you better pay your bill? You should always pay for what you take." The thin man chuckled and he patted his friend with appreciation at this remark.

Prakash headed towards the cashier at the front of the cafe, the two men rising from their chairs to follow him. He looked around wildly, wondering if he could make a run for it, but knew that it was hopeless. They were standing close to him, shadowing his shoulders and would grab him if he tried to escape. The men took his arms as they left Cafe Madras and led him to a car, opening the rear door and manoeuvring him into the back seat. He fought back panic and felt tears pricking his eyes.

"What do you want?" he whispered.

The big man turned to look at him over his shoulder and shook his head. He had heard it all before. There would be denials, then protests of innocence, but then he would break and tell them the truth. They all did in the end and he often wondered why they had to be so predictable. Why they had to go through this game when they could just save him the effort of threats and assault and just confess all straight away? He turned to his friend and nodded, and the thin man leaned around and struck Prakash hard in the face.

"Don't take us for fools," he said before pulling away from the kerb.

Prakash sat in the back of the car, the fingers of his hands twisting around each other, his teeth clenched and his heart pounding. The engine stopped and the men opened the door, pulling him out of the car and leading him towards a row of shops in a neighbourhood he was unfamiliar with. They entered a general store, the shelves stacked close together, piled high with stock. The man behind the counter looked up, registered the two men and waggled his head nervously in acknowledgement.

"We're going to make use of your basement," the big man said.

The owner's face was a picture of fear as he bobbled his head

106

again and returned to his work.

The basement was small and filled with boxes of supplies piled in stacks around the room. The big man pushed Prakash onto a low stool while the thin man pulled a wadge of cable ties from his pocket that he handed to his companion who swiftly and deftly linked them together to lengthen them so that he could secure each leg to the legs of the stool, then moved behind Prakash to bind his wrists behind his back.

The big man looked at Prakash, his face darkening as he leaned over and hit him hard on the mouth. The stool rocked to one side under the force of the thwack but his friend reached his hands forward to catch Prakash's shoulders.

Prakash felt a warm trickle down the side of his lip. He opened his mouth to ask what this was all about, who were they and what did they want, but remembered the menacing words that had answered him in the car, "don't take us for fools…"

He closed his mouth and waited, his heart pounding in his chest, the sound resounding in his ears.

"My boss thinks you were friendly with someone he knew." Prakash looked up at the big man, his eyes wide with surprise.

"Arundhati," he said. "Is that right? Were you friendly with a woman called… Arundhati?" He brought his face close to Prakash, his eyes boring into him.

Prakash nodded, the sweat trickling down his neck forming rivulets down his body and under his arms.

"Good." The big man rose heavily. "She had something valuable that belonged to our boss and it's gone missing. We think you might be able to help us. I hope for your sake you can." He grinned menacingly.

Prakash felt his bowels loosen with fear. He gulped.

"Did Arundhati tell you what she did with the diamonds?"

107

Prakash knitted his eyebrows together. "Diamonds? What diamonds?" he asked, his voice quivering with fear.

The big man stepped forwards and struck him hard on the cheek. His head whipped round to the side, his cheekbone inflamed and burning.

"I asked you a question," the big man stated flatly. "Where are the diamonds?"

Prakash racked his brain, frantically searching for an answer that would satisfy these men and prevent them from hurting him further.

"I don't know anything about diamonds." Prakash's brain swirled in desperation to give them an answer that would be satisfactory. " She... she sent me a package in the post to look after, but it was a locket, not diamonds. A locket that I had given her a year ago. I put it in the drawer next to my bed, but it's gone. I checked."

The two men grinned and came closer to him. "Who cares about a locket? I asked you about diamonds."

Prakash stared at them, his eyes wide with fear. "I told you, I don't know anything about diamonds." Frustration rose within him. "Was it you who ransacked my flat? If so, you must know that I have no diamonds."

The thin man thwacked him hard across the back and Prakash felt a loss of oxygen. He gasped for breath. There was another hard punch to his abdomen. Flashing lights appeared behind his eyelids as searing pain twisted through his body.

"You have something that doesn't belong to you," the big man said, leaning into Prakash. "Something that belongs to our boss. It's not clever to steal from our boss," he growled, the snarl curling the corner of his lip.

"I didn't steal from anybody," he gasped. "I came home and

my flat was destroyed – by you... I know nothing about diamonds."

The two men looked at each other.

"We've got all day and I don't mind how long it takes, but it would be easier for you if you told us sooner rather than later where the diamonds are." The big man nodded to his friend who sliced through the cable tie, releasing Prakash's arms. The thin man lifted up one arm and held it.

"Now where are they?"

Prakash gathered his fractured strength and opened his mouth, relieved to hear he still had the use of his voice. "If I had any diamonds, you would have found them when you turned my flat upside down. The only thing I got from Arundhati was a locket, but someone took that when they destroyed my flat. Wasn't it you?" he whispered. "Please believe me."

"The flat was ransacked before we got there. If we had the diamonds, why would we be asking you where they are? And I have no idea why you think we are interested in a bloody locket," the big man spat.

Prakash looked up in surprise.

The thin man grabbed Prakash's arm and in one swift movement, it was wrenched out and back forcefully and he heard the snap before he felt it.

"Where are the diamonds?" the thin man whispered into Prakash's ear.

Prakash felt himself submerged in a whirlpool of pain that threatened to drown him. His ears were filled with strange subterranean sounds through which he could just make out a distant voice forming what sounded like words. But he couldn't make any sense of them.

"Where are the diamonds?" The man said again.

With great difficulty he felt his lips form an answer, his voice barely issuing any sound.

Prakash's eyes squeezed together tightly in preparation for the next onslaught.

"The person who ransacked the flat and robbed the locket must have them," he moaned.

His head rolled back and he looked away and waited. Who would have thought that he would die in the basement of an unknown shop like this? Was this his karma for the life he had led? Darkness entered him and he knew nothing.

Chapter 17
Mumbai 2018

Ajay was on his 28th lap. He was a powerful swimmer, and his bulk moved through the water with force as though he were conquering any resistance he might meet, creating waves that sent the water overflowing the infinity pool. Like many people, Ajay thought best when he performed repetitive movements that allowed his mind freedom to roam and ponder. Some people walked. Ajay swam. His thoughts returned once again to the missing diamonds. It wasn't the loss of their worth that bothered him. Arundhati had been clever enough to have stalled suspicion by handing over the majority of the diamonds, only keeping a few back and it had taken a while before the discrepancy had been noticed. What bothered him were the unanswered questions and the potential threat those questions posed to his organisation. Arundhati had sent a locket to her gay friend, Prakash, before she had been killed by somebody unknown. Why had she done that? And why had someone ransacked the flat and taken the locket?

Ajay let out a snort that reverberated under water. The thief had probably taken a liking to it and decided to give it as a present to his wife, mistress or daughter. His mind turned back to Arundhati. She had become increasingly demanding, but had she planned on blackmailing him? And who had killed her? Had the person who had killed her done so for the diamonds, and if so, did they have the diamonds? Or was somebody else involved? The murder had happened in Antwerp, but the ransacking had been in Mumbai – was there a link? His legs pushed off the side of the pool vigorously as he spun his body round to complete another lap.

He disliked being robbed, but even more worrying was a potential threat to him and his business. Could it be a rival gang muscling in… or a new upstart perhaps making his presence felt. He clenched his jaw and felt anger boil within him, sending his heart racing. Reaching the side of the pool, he flipped over onto his back, his stomach rising like a beached whale, and closed his eyes. He needed to keep calm in order to think clearly, and he was due to meet with Mansingh this morning to find out how the investigations with that actress woman had progressed. Ajay floated effortlessly and felt himself relax. Nobody was going to undermine his empire. He was Ajay 'Baalon Vaala' Bhatwedekar. He laughed at the nickname that had been given to him as a young man – 'the hairy one'– and stroked his stomach. Maybe his hair was his secret weapon, his strength.

Cape Town 2015

Arundhati sank back into her pillows, her feet outstretched on the hotel bed. It had been just another flight, another long day at work, this time from Paris where she had been lucky enough to have had a day off to shop. She had had Ajay very much in mind as she had headed to the Rue Cambon to enter the luxurious world of Cadolle Lingerie. She wanted to wear something special next time he undressed her. Much to her surprise, Arundhati had felt slightly intimidated entering the boutique, despite the professional Parisian welcome she had received. Or was it because of it? She had not experienced racism until she had entered the world of air travel. Up till then, she had never been outside of India. It was not as though the colour of a person's skin

112

didn't matter at home. 'Fair and Lovely' skin whitening products abounded, and a bride was more highly prized the lighter her complexion. But Arundhati had never given the matter much consideration, as she herself had always been complimented on the shade and tone of her skin, which was a light olive brown. Her experience of prejudice in Ahmedabad was more to do with religion and caste than anything else. So it was with surprise that she realised upon entering the global world of air travel that some people considered her inferior just because she was Indian. Even worse, she was aware that the derogatory term 'Paki' was directed towards her because of the way she looked and the colour of her skin. She was astonished that people could mistake her for a Pakistani. Growing up in Gujarat, she was conditioned to have a suspicious loathing of Pakistan. She wanted to tell them that they were mistaken in their assumption, that she was Indian and that she too disliked the people of Pakistan.

She had steeled herself to be assertive on this shopping expedition and had thought carefully about her image. Paris was renowned for its fashion and she had travelled enough to have refined her dress sense. She wore skin tight black jeans over high heels, a silk turmeric coloured top and a square cut black jacket. Her long black hair was styled in loose waves that fell around her shoulders and her makeup was impeccably applied. However, when she entered the shop and saw the shop assistants' eyes scan her from top to toe, her confidence wavered. It didn't help that she spoke very little French, though she had practised her vocabulary for this particular expedition.

Arundhati lifted her chin and emulated the autocratic manner many of the passengers assumed when travelling business class.

"*Bonjour, je veux de lingerie s'il vous plaît.*"

The shop assistant, her hair slicked back into a neat low

ponytail, nodded and pursed her cherry red lips.

"Quelle taille avez-vous besoin?"

Arundhati's eyebrows furrowed as her brain sought to decipher the question. The woman sighed extravagantly, and in a thick French accent repeated the question in English, "What size do you 'ave?"

Arundhati smiled gratefully and answered, then explained what she wanted. The shop assistant gave her another all over body scan, nodded as though in agreement, then moved swiftly and efficiently, her well-manicured finger skimming the shelves, running over the boxes and pulling out a selection of lingerie. Arundhati squealed with delight at the delicate beauty of the undergarments, one more exquisite than the next and bit her lip, aware that she was going to be paying a high price for these flimsy little items. But what had she expected coming into Cadolle; this was lingerie for the stars, for royalty, and for Arundhati, it was an investment in her future with Ajay. She selected a seductive bra with matching briefs in a stunning rose and gold coloured silk, trimmed with lace and brought out her card, inserting it into the machine swiftly. She had never indulged herself in such extravagance, but it would be worth it.

The shop assistant smiled professionally, complimenting her on her choice. She was satisfied and Arundhati was gratified as she left proudly carrying the small bag bearing the name Cadolle.

Arundhati drew the box containing the precious items closer towards her on the bed. She lifted the lid and gently peeled back the tissue wrapping to reveal the lingerie. Her fingers stroked the silk with awe. She folded the paper back again and closed the box. It would remain in perfect condition until the time she wore them for Ajay.

There was a knock on the hotel room door and Arundhati rose to answer it. A man stood outside in the corridor, a parcel in his hands. "Mademoiselle Adani?'

She nodded and he placed the package in her hands and walked away.

Puzzled, she returned to sit on the edge of the bed and unpeeled the tape. Inside was a bra and she gasped at the unexpected weight as her fingers lifted it. So it was finally happening. This was it. She undressed quickly and tried it on. It was a perfect fit, the gems embedded like oversized diamanté trimmings.

Her hands stroked them with awe. Compared to the delicate bra she had just bought, this one felt like a workhorse, but it was comfortable enough. The cups were well padded to accommodate the shape and bulk of the diamonds, the face of the gems decorating the edge of her breasts. It would work. She was ready.

She rose early the next morning after a fitful night's sleep, her mind envisaging the various potential scenarios that could come into play during the journey from Cape Town to Mumbai tomorrow.

She had bought a more opaque vest to cover the bra underneath her thin uniform blouse. Turning fiom side to side, she nodded approval. It reassured her that Priya would be on the same flight. It would normalise the situation and take her mind off what she was about to do. They met down in the lobby as usual and sat next to each other on the airport bus to the terminal, completing the journey in silence. It was six a.m., everyone had done this journey many times before and at that time in the morning there was little need to talk. As Arundhati neared security, she felt her heart race, her mouth become dry and her stomach felt like a troupe of miniature acrobats had installed themselves and were rehearsing flips and jumps on a trampoline on her spleen. She was well aware of how well security were trained at sensing tension, noticing awkward self-conscious discomfort. The last thing she wanted was to exude panic and attract attention.

"Are you OK? You've been very quiet this morning and you look a bit feverish," Priya asked her with some concern in her expression.

Arundhati gulped and reached for a tissue, dabbing the moisture from her upper lip, taking the opportunity to pause and regulate her breath. She turned to Priya and managed a smile, then changing the subject she said brightly, "I went shopping yesterday and bought some lingerie. Beautiful French lingerie."

Priya raised her eyebrows. "Lingerie, is it? When in France..." She gave her a knowing look. "Is this for Prakash's benefit?"

Arundhati shrugged, her eyes raised to the ceiling in a mock expression of thought and felt herself relax. She continued walking and said, "Maybe, maybe not... I'll see how he behaves..." and she threw her head back, releasing a peal of laughter just as they passed through security.

"I'll have some of that," the man chuckled as she passed him. Arundhati threw him a smile. She had done it. It had worked.

Mumbai 2018

Ajay gestured to Mansingh to take a seat and clicked his fingers for the boy to pour the hot drinks, masala chai for Mansingh and filter coffee for himself.

He sat in his armchair of choice, one ankle crossed over the other knee, his elbows resting on the arms of the chair, fingertips gently touching. He nodded in approval and then gestured for the boy to leave with a sweep of his hand.

"So," he began, "what can you tell me about this actress? What does she know?"

Mansingh leaned towards the cup and lifted the chai to his lips. Whoever made it knew what they were doing. The perfect blend of spices, cardamom, ginger, black pepper and not too much jaggery sweetness, just as he liked it. He waggled his head in approval.

"I'm not sure how much she knows, but I know she does not have the diamonds." He paused, looking directly at Ajay. "She has questions and is keen to know more, and with the right encouragement, she might find the answers."

Ajay tapped his fingertips together and grunted, considering Mansingh's words. "Do we want her to know more?" he asked.

Mansingh smiled. "So long as we are in control of what she knows, then it could be to our advantage that she does the digging – not us. That way we stay in the background, but get the information."

Ajay nodded thoughtfully.

Mansingh continued. "I have gained her trust. She is at a tipping point between deciding whether to return to her holiday, or get more involved. Jitu and Vasant scared her, but I can see her wondering why Prakash had his flat ransacked and is wondering what they were looking for. I think it would be easy to encourage her probe further."

Ajay raised his eyebrows questioningly. "And when she finds out?"

Mansingh laughed softly. "When she finds out, we'll have what's been stolen from you and our lovely actress friend will have an unfortunate accident."

Ajay smiled. "Good. I know I can trust you to handle her." He stood up and reached an arm out for Mansingh, giving him an affectionate hug. "I want this sorted as quickly as possible, but you are right, it needs to be done with care. I must find out who is responsible and cut the head off the snake swiftly. I don't want a spotlight on my business. OK?"

Mansingh gripped Ajay's arm and waggled his head in affirmation. "I understand, boss. I'll see to it."

Chapter 18
Mumbai 2018

Indy closed the lid on her suitcase and sat down to double check her documents. Passport, check; phone fully charged with e-ticket to Ahmedabad, check; phone charger, check. She gave the bedroom another scan to make sure nothing had been forgotten under the bed, in the drawers and cupboard, lastly entering the bathroom. Done.

A smile spread across her face as she thought about her forthcoming adventure. She felt slightly nervous and excited about Mansingh's invitation and she wondered whether to read anything into it. She reminded herself that invitations were more spontaneous, casual and forthcoming in India than in the UK, where you often had to know someone for years before being asked into their home. He hadn't suggested she stayed with him, much to her relief.

Given that they hadn't been physical with each other at all, that would have been disconcerting, but it seemed to her that there was an electricity between them that suggested more than just a friendship and she hadn't felt that buzz in a long time. It was a good feeling.

She had organised Sandeep to take her to the airport where she would meet Mansingh. It was on her bucket list to take the legendary Indian trains, but Mansingh had explained to her that not only was India a very large country with very slow trains, but the booking system was over complicated. It was necessary to book in advance as there were 'wait' times that meant you waited to see if seats would be released and available. He had also stressed how much quicker it was to fly so she had acquiesced, deciding that she would organise a train trip in the future – though, she mused, it would have been nice to have had company on a long journey.

Indira gathered her belongings and took the lift down to the hotel lobby. She had fifteen minutes until her cab came, but she was ready to go and disliked hanging around. She was settling the bill for her stay when the phone rang and she saw to her surprise it was Sonal.

"Hello, Sonal, how are you?" she asked cautiously. Indy remembered that the last time they had spoken she had been sure that Sonal had lied to her.

"Indy, I'm fine. Are you having a good time in India?" Her voice sounded stilted and Indy paused. Indy felt instinctively there was something wrong.

"I'm having a lovely time, Sonal. Is everything all right with you? Prakash must be back with you. How is he?"

There was a long silence at the other end of the call and Indy looked to see if they had been cut off. No, the screen showed the call was still active.

"Sonal, are you there?"

"Yes, I am here, but I need your help. I don't know what to do." Her words hung in the air and Indy stepped in to fill the space.

"Tell me what's happened, Sonal."

"Prakash came home, but he's... he's..." Indira heard Sonal's voice struggling to speak.

"He's what, Sonal? Take a deep breath. Is he OK?"

"I think somebody attacked him and beat him up. His arm is

broken and he looks a mess. He says it was an accident, but I don't believe it. I don't know what to do... What should I do?"

Indy's thoughts drifted immediately to the two men who had threatened her in Prakash's flat. They had been looking for something. Did Prakash have what they were looking for?

Were they responsible for attacking Prakash? If so, then she couldn't help thinking that he was lucky they had let him go and he was still alive.

However, there was no reason to alarm Sonal further so she just said, "That's terrible news, Sonal. But he says he was in an accident. Why would you think it was anything else? Why would he make that up?"

The voice at the other end of the phone noticeably increased in volume and Indira looked towards the receptionist with an apologetic smile.

"Why would I think he is lying? He's been lying to me for years – about that other woman. I know something has happened and I want you to find out what it is!"

Indira closed her eyes, wishing that she had never answered this call. This trip to Ahmedabad was important to her and she had closed the door on pretending to be a real detective to keep Sonal happy.

"Sonal, I'm on my way to Ahmedabad. Prakash is back with you and for the sake of your relationship, I think it's time for you both to be straight with each other. Listen, I need to catch my flight, but I will call you soon. I promise." She clicked off before Sonal could reply and saw Sandeep enter the lobby. She threw him a smile and followed him out of the hotel and into the cab.

Sinking back into the familiar seat, she let her gaze soften as she looked out of the side window of the taxi. As Sandeep drove down the Mumbai streets, the images merged and flowed into each other, her eyes no longer aware of what they were seeing. Her thoughts retreated as her mind reviewed past events; the ransacked flat, the two men, her fear at what they might do to her and now Prakash's injuries. She felt a wave of guilt that Sonal had called her for help and she had been dismissive, thinking only of herself and her trip to Ahmedabad. And Mansingh...

She groaned inadvertently and Sandeep looked into the rearview mirror. "Everything OK, ma'am?"

Indy nodded. "Everything is fine, Sandeep." She smiled. "I'm just a nervous flyer."

Sandeep's reflection grinned at her. "Don't worry, ma'am. I will say a puja for you and Krishna will take care of you." He gestured towards the small figure of a man, standing on one leg, the other casually crossed as he played a flute, and touched it gently, then touched his forehead and heart. "I say a puja every morning before driving my taxicab, and look, I am still here," he said, his smile increasing as he returned his gaze to the road just in time to avoid a man weaving his way between the traffic.

"Great," Indy replied, laughing. "Just don't rely only on Krishna, help him out a bit and keep an eye on the road yourself."

Sandeep grinned, waggling his head enthusiastically. "Yes, ma'am."

He pulled up at Mumbai airport and Indy gave him a generous tip, promising to contact him if she returned to the city, and also promising to tell others about his wonderful service.

Sandeep waggled his head happily, looking genuinely touched by her kindness and expressing sorrow that she was leaving.

Mansingh was waiting for her and after they had passed through the endless queues and document checks that began even before they entered the airport building, they finally settled down to wait for their flight.

"Are you all right?" she heard him ask her. She had been drifting in and out of her thoughts, feeling guilty that she hadn't helped Sonal and roused herself.

"Yes, sorry, Mansingh. I was just..." She hesitated, unsure of how much to tell him. Shaking her head as though to wake herself, she smiled. "I was just daydreaming."

The flight was short and uneventful, and they landed in Ahmedabad airport on time. Collecting their luggage, they were heading out of the airport when Indy suddenly stopped and turned to Mansingh.

"Will you give me a minute, please? I just want to check something out. Can we go to the Qatar Airlines check-in desks? I'll explain later."

Mansingh nodded. "Of course."

Walking towards the Qatar desks, Indira was berating herself for being drawn in again. What were the chances of anyone knowing Arundhati and being able to tell her something – anything – of use? But despite these doubts, she heard herself asking a woman in a burgundy uniform, "Can I have a moment of your time? I was wondering if you, or anyone here, might have known Arundhati Adani? I just wanted to ask a couple of questions – and, of course, give my condolences."

The woman looked at her suspiciously and then said, "Are you with the police?"

Indy's jaw dropped in surprise. She had been unaware that she had been channelling

Inspector Rose McKinley. She shook her head vehemently and laughed lightly. "No! No, I'm just a... friend..."

The flight attendant paused, then nodded. "Just a minute,"

she said before turning on her heels towards another woman, also dressed in burgundy. Indy saw the woman turn to look at her with a puzzled expression before walking towards her.

"Can I help you?" she asked.

Indy nodded. "You were a friend of Arundhati's?" Her voice and manner softer than before. A waggle of the head was the response.

"I'm so sorry for your loss. I hope you don't mind me asking you a couple of questions, but I'm a friend of Prakash's."

The woman's eyes showed clearly that she understood who Prakash was.

Indy persevered. "Prakash was beaten up quite badly recently. This may sound strange, but I am wondering if there is any possibility there is a link to what happened to Arundhati and the assault on Prakash. Did you notice anything from what Arundhati said or did recently that might help?"

The woman's eyes were scanning Indy's face intently while she spoke, and it seemed she had come to a decision because she reached out her hand to introduce herself.

"My name is Priya. Can I ask what is your good name, please?" Indy answered, and Priya continued.

"Arundhati and I were good friends. You know she was having an affair with Prakash?" Indy nodded.

"I told her many times that I thought it was a foolish thing to do. A waste of her time, but she just laughed at me and told me not to take life so seriously. She said she didn't care about the affair as much as Prakash did – he was crazy about her, she told me."

Indy registered this information and continued, "It seems that there is something missing that people want. These people have threatened Prakash and I am wondering if there is a link between what they are looking for and what happened to Arundhati. I don't suppose you know anything about it?"

Priya shook her head, her eyebrows furrowed. "No... but the last couple of years, I saw less and less of Arundhati. She was always busy. Our hours can be crazy, but we used to spend time together after work, you know, to unwind. Then she began to make excuses and when I asked what she was doing, she just shrugged and didn't say. If I hadn't known she was having an affair with Prakash, I would have thought she was seeing someone else – someone with a lot of money."

Indy raised her eyebrows questioningly.

"When she wasn't in uniform, she dressed expensively – well, it looked like it anyway. And..." She stopped and bit her lip.

"And?"

"Well, I saw her open her bag once, and there was an envelope full of bills. Big bills."

"Did you ask her about it?" Indy probed.

Priya shook her head. "No. Maybe I didn't want to know." She smiled ruefully. "I'm sorry, I had better get back to work. I hope I've been some help."

Indy nodded appreciatively. "You have. Thank you so much. And once again, I'm really sorry about what happened to Arundhati."

Priya nodded and turned back to the desk, then said, "Oh, just a minute" and turned her head towards Indy. She walked swiftly to the desk and moved behind it. Reaching down, she then emerged with a set of keys.

"Arundhati gave me a set of keys to her flat in case I ever needed a place to stay or if she ever lost hers. I don't think many people knew about it. I wouldn't feel like staying there now, but you might find some answers there." She handed over the keys with a rueful smile, and then produced a card. "This is my contact number if you need to get hold of me for any reason. I hope you find out who murdered Arundhati." Her large brown eyes looked into Indy's and began to fill with tears. "She was my friend," she said softly, and turned away.

Indy put the card into her purse and turned to Mansingh who had been standing at a respectful distance away from her.

Gazing at the keys in amazement, she held them out carefully as though they were precious treasure and whispered with stifled excitement, "I've got the keys to Arundhati's flat!"

Mansingh guided Indy out of the airport with a smile.

Chapter 19
Goa 2018

Arundhati stood in the en suite shower enjoying the cascade of hot water that gushed over her, washing away the stagnant air of the business class cabin that permeated her body. She had learned that whether it was business class or economy class, the air remained the same, there were just fewer people sharing it. This was her last flight for a while and she was going to enjoy a few days' break with Ajay at his home in Goa, something she was very much looking forward to. Her flight destinations had worked out in his favour recently, taking her from Harare to Cape Town and Antwerp in quick succession, earning herself quite a healthy income, but she realised that she had seen very little of Ajay himself over the last couple of months – a situation that concerned her. She knew she was useful, but she wanted to be more than that. Arundhati was not ready to return to her former life of mediocrity. She had tasted wealth and power, and she wanted her share on a more permanent basis. She smiled to herself and stroked the palms of her hands down her body. She was looking forward to seeing Ajay.

Stepping out of the shower, she reached for the towels, wrapping one around her freshly washed hair, the other around her body, taking for granted the ease and comfort of a hotel where everything was always available, ready and waiting for her use.

Her phone rang and she saw Priya's name appear on the

screen. She had seen comparatively little of Priya outside of work, but she could rectify that tonight.

"Hi, Priya!" she responded with warmth.

"Arundhati," came the reply. "Some of us are meeting downstairs in the bar for a drink tonight at eight. Do you want to join us?"

Arundhati felt momentary disappointment that Priya had made plans with others before calling her first, but quickly put that to one side. It would be fun to see everyone.

"Of course. I look forward to it."

She woke the next morning and reached for the paracetamol. It felt like someone had hit her over the head with a hammer repeatedly during the night. Arundhati rolled over in bed and groaned. It had been a fun night though. She had forgotten how much she enjoyed socialising with the crew, people with shared experiences and stories. There had been an awkward moment when Ajay's name had come up and one of the girls had teased her about 'the chemistry' between them, but she had shaken it off, saying that she was in a relationship already. Prakash was proving to be a good alibi, though only Priya knew that he was married and she hadn't told Priya that it had been a long time since she had actually seen him. She had caught Priya looking at her and returned the look with an innocent expression on her face and just for a moment she wondered what was going through Priya's mind.

A car was waiting for her as she left Dabolim Airport in Goa. Ajay hadn't turned up to welcome her, but then she hadn't expected him to be there in person. He was too successful to have time for romantic gestures like that, and she had to admit that it was one of the things she liked about him. He put business first and the knowledge that he had built up a successful empire thrilled her. She had a small slice of it and before long she was going to increase her portion.

The car drove through the electric gates down a long driveway towards Ajay's house overlooking the sea, finally pulling up in front of the mansion. The driver stepped out to open the door for Arundhati, a gesture that she barely acknowledged as she walked towards the front door.

Security was as tight here as it was at his house in Mumbai. Walking into Ajay's homes was like walking through airport security. Pockets were emptied, phones were confiscated, and bodies were scanned. Ajay was no fool. He knew how easy it would be to ensnare him and he made sure that both his homes had a faraday cage around them and that all business conversations that involved his name happened within his own walls. Anyone breaching this protocol was dealt with severely as a warning to others.

A manservant appeared from nowhere to collect her bags and he followed her into the large marbled entrance hall. She was used to the drill. The butler would arrive and either show her to the bedroom or announce her to Ajay, depending on whether Ajay was busy or not.

She threw an inquiring look at Motes, the butler, to see which it would be and he gestured for her to stay. Ajay was free to see her.

Kicking off her shoes, she glanced at her reflection in the ornate mirror that hung in the large entrance lobby and arranged her hair, then glancing briefly at her body, she reached down into her plunge bra to pull up her breasts, stretching the low cut top down over them to reveal as much as possible. Quickly reapplying her lipstick, she turned in response to Motes beckoning her to follow him to the rear of the house and walked down the hall towards the large French doors that opened out onto the patio, garden and pool.

Ajay reclined on his lounger, his eyes shaded by sunglasses, a glass of whisky in his hand. Arundhati leaned over to kiss him, her breasts lightly brushing past his face. He grabbed her, the whisky pouring over them as he buried his face in between her soft mounds.

"Ajay! My clothes will be ruined!"

Immediately, he ripped her top apart and she gasped at the violence. "I am sure you are earning enough to buy another," he replied.

She pouted then kissed him again. "You tore it so you should replace it."

He let out a belly laugh and smacked her hard on the buttocks. "That's what I like about you, Arundhati. You say what you think. Sure, I will buy you another. I might rip the skirt off you too."

She struggled to extricate herself from his grasp. "Why don't I just take it off myself? I'm quite fond of this one."

Ajay grinned. "Maybe we shouldn't give the servants too much enjoyment. Go and slip on a bikini and come back to me."

Arundhati returned wearing a large brimmed hat and a beautifully embroidered long kaftan to shield herself from the sun. He frowned at the outfit and growled, "I said a bikini."

She removed the hat and slipped the kaftan down around her ankles, stepping out of it to show her bikini and placing her hands on her hips provocatively. "You don't want me to get dark-skinned, do you?" she asked with a smile.

Signalling for another glass of whisky, he said, "Get in the pool."

She frowned. "You know I can't swim."

Ajay nodded. "I know. Maybe it's time you learned. Get in the water."

Arundhati looked at him, then shrugged. Turning to the pool, she threw herself into the deep end. He sat up quickly and watched the surface ripples, waiting for her to re-emerge. Her face appeared, hands flapping furiously, mouth gasping for air. Laughing, he jumped in beside her, his massive body creating waves that sent the water overflowing the pool as he reached for her, supporting her in the water.

"You're a crazy woman, you know that? Come on, we'll get you a drink."

Arundhati lay on the large double bed unable to sleep. Ajay had been as enthusiastic as ever in his sexual demands. He liked to dominate, but he enjoyed a participatory partner who was active in the bedroom and enjoyed sex as much as he did. Passiveness did not appeal to Ajay. Arundhati was more than happy to comply and over the two years she had known Ajay, she had learned how to pleasure him to his great satisfaction. There was nothing passive about Arundhati. The question she was mulling over in her head right now was how far could she assert herself, not just in the bedroom, but in their relationship. She flipped back the sheet that covered her naked body and rose from the bed, walking towards the sliding glass doors that led to the terrace overlooking the sea. Parting the doors, she slipped outside, feeling the warm and gentle breeze fluttering delicately over her skin and she closed her eyes, inhaling the intoxicating scent from the flowers in the garden below. She leaned her arms on the terrace railing, leaning into the darkness and not for the first time pondered how to manage her ambition. She wanted this life. She wanted it with every fibre of her body; the house, the servants, the money, and Ajay was the key. He could give it to her, she just had to make sure that he chose her.

She rolled round, leaning her back on the balustrade, her eyes scanning the house. It was a magnificent modern construction that made the most of the panoramic views around it. Huge glass bulletproof windows were placed at every level, with doors opening onto terraces, sheltered from the sun by retractable canopies. Arundhati smiled as she realised that Ajay's bedroom and en suite was probably the floorspace of her parents' entire apartment. Something small and pink caught her eyes to the right of the terrace and she walked over to satisfy her curiosity. Squatting down, she felt the anger within her rise to boiling as she held the delicate briefs in her fingers. Turning abruptly, she walked back to the bed and placed them on Ajay's face before rolling over onto her side and closing her eyes.

Ajay awoke, his fingers brushing a strange item from his nose. Slowly opening his eyes, he gradually realised what it was that was dangling in front of him. Shit. How had they arrived on his face?

He glanced over at Arundhati, who lay fast asleep beside him. She must have found them – but when? He hadn't noticed her leaving the bed last night, but there was no other explanation. He clenched his teeth and threw them disdainfully to the floor.

As he heaved himself out of bed, Arundhati turned and looked at him. He returned her stare, raising one eyebrow as though inviting her to challenge him. She turned away and walked to the bathroom wordlessly. Her anger and everything she had wanted to say to him last night choked in her throat.

Ajay smiled and rubbed his belly with satisfaction. Hearing

a rush of water, he realised she must be having a shower and he entered the bathroom feeling his penis rise with desire. Sex in the morning was a perfect way to start the day.

The air was filled with steam as he moved towards the large area that was partially divided by glass, behind which Arundhati was standing under a cascade of water. His hands reached for her hips from behind and she elbowed him hard. Ajay gasped with surprise, momentarily losing his grip.

She spun round, her face reddened with anger, as she spat out the words "Don't touch me."

Ajay's expression darkened as he growled, "I'll touch you if I want." He moved towards her and very deliberately placed his hands firmly on her hips.

She glared at him as she stated in an accusatory voice, "You've been having sex with another woman."

He smiled menacingly. "I'll have sex with whoever I want, whenever I want – including you, Arundhati," and he came closer. She tugged at his hands to free herself and he lifted his hand to strike her.

"You would hit the mother of your baby?"

Ajay's arm paused and he lowered it slowly, staring at her, his mouth moving as if to form words, but no sound came forth.

She smiled, her eyes glittering. "I was going to tell you this weekend."

He walked out of the bathroom and she watched him, wrapping a towel around herself. He turned slowly towards her and said with suspicion in this voice, "How do I know it's mine? You've been seeing that man Prakash. My men told me."

Arundhati looked at him in surprise. Of course, she would have been watched. She phrased her words carefully, "You know I see him. He's my cover for our relationship. Yes, I have seen him, but I haven't slept with him. He's gay, I told you that."

Ajay's eyes narrowed. "He's married with a child. Doesn't sound very gay to me."

Arundhati chortled. "Really? You don't think half the men in India who are married with children are really homosexual? Come on, Ajay. You know people in India can't be openly gay. Being married with children is the perfect cover."

Ajay grunted.

"I'll pay for an abortion and that will be the end of it," he said flatly.

Arundhati sat on an armchair and crossed her legs. This was not the intended outcome.

"I don't want an abortion. I want your baby, Ajay," she purred. "That's why I was so unhappy that you were with someone else."

Slowly, she moved towards him, her towel unravelling. "I make you happy, Ajay, and I'm good at my work, aren't I?" She threw him a dazzling smile as she caressed him. "We could be a team, you and I. You wouldn't regret it."

Ajay allowed himself to be pushed onto his back and accepted Arundhati's apology with increasing pleasure. She was certainly good at what she did, but he had no plans to make her a permanent feature in his world. Something would have to be done.

Chapter 20
Ahmedabad 2018

Indy stood outside her hotel waiting for Mansingh to arrive. The city was hot and dry, the dusty air heavy. In front of her, the road teamed with traffic loudly honking their horns, nose to nose, three lanes in each direction, motorbikes and people weaving randomly between the cars. It was like a game with the only rule being not to touch one another, the penalty being that if you hit someone, you lose points and if you get hit, you die.

An auto rickshaw u-turned in front of her against the traffic flow and she saw Mansingh's head pop out of the open doorway, his face smiling at her as he waved hello. She walked towards him, stooping to get inside and sat next to him underneath the plastic covered face of Arundhati Roy who beamed at her from the ceiling.

"First stop, Teen Darwaja," he told her enthusiastically.

Indy smiled, feeling relaxed and secure in Mansingh's care. "Whatever that is, sounds wonderful."

She placed her bag beside her and felt Mansingh's arm reach over to lift it onto her lap.

"Keep hold of your belongings, there are no doors," he said quietly.

She looked up to see the driver adjust his mirror so that he could watch her while he was driving. Rear-view mirrors were obviously an unnecessary inconvenience when the choice was between looking at traffic or female passengers. She stared back at him until he averted his eyes and then turned her head to peer out of the open doorway to her side. The rickshaw came to a stop at a red traffic light and suddenly a crowd of children gathered in front of her face with outstretched hands, pulling at her clothes and gesturing with pursed fingers to their mouths indicating hunger. She reeled back in her seat in surprise, clutching her bag and fingers to Mansingh. "I should give them some money…"

Mansingh placed his hand on top of hers. "Look at their fingers," he said, his eyes indicating towards their hands. "The third and fourth fingers of their hands are fused together. They are like bonded slaves. Any money you give them will go back to their gang master."

Indy stared at him in horror as Mansingh shouted at them and they left with a raucous laugh.

She slumped back in her seat despondently.

"There are plenty of people to give money to in this city," he stated in a matter-of-fact way. "Old people on the streets, orphanages. Don't worry, if you want to be generous, there is no shortage of charitable cases. Let's not feed the bad guys, *eh*?" He lowered his head to peer out and gestured to the driver to stop, "Bas, bas, here is good."

They stepped out of the rickshaw into a melee of people pushing their way in all directions, shoulder to shoulder, each with their own sense of purpose. Ahead of them was a huge stone wall with a triple archway through which she could see endless stalls.

Mansingh turned to her with a grin. "Teen Darwaja, the triple gate, and the heart of Ahmedabad's shopping district – unless, of course, you prefer to go to the malls and shopping centres."

Indy shook her head slowly, her eyes filled with wonder.

"This is a huge bazaar where you can find anything and

everything. Hardware, clothes, fabrics, food, jewellery... what do you want? Within Teenn Darwaja there are neighbourhoods for each section. Jewellery? Saris?"

She looked at him helplessly. "Let's just walk through it," she answered breathlessly.

He nodded. "Stick close to me," he directed as they forged into the crowd.

Mansingh obviously knew the bazaar like the back of his hand, an ability that seemed incredible to her as she followed him down a network of alleyways that meandered, winding circuitously in all directions so that very soon she was completely disorientated. The contents of the shops spilled outside, tempting customers to enter, the goods often dangling from strings and awnings in front of her face as she attempted to make her way down the alleys, weaving between people and stalls, finding it hard to keep track of Mansingh. There were so many people everywhere, all around her, and she felt a rising panic at the thought of losing him and being left to find her own way out of this impenetrable maze. A hand grabbed her arm and pulled her towards the wall behind her.

"Careful!"

She gasped as three huge beautifully painted elephants squeezed down the narrow alleyway, their mahouts sitting proudly astride the necks of the animals, waving long sticks.

The crowd seemed to pay no particular heed to the inconvenience this caused, moving aside just enough to allow the elephants through before continuing as before.

Indy turned to look at Mansingh. "I can't believe I just saw real elephants walking down the street! I'm so excited!"

"I can tell," he replied with a smile. "They are temple elephants, used for festivals mostly. Come, we are heading to

Badshah's Tomb and my favourite shop."

She followed him closely down the vennels, finally emerging into a wider street. He gestured towards a shop.

"Gamthiwalah," he said with satisfaction. "The best fabrics in town." Slipping off his sandals, he gestured to her to do the same and they were greeted warmly by a striking man sitting cross legged on the floor, his eyes rimmed with kohl and dressed in an unfashionably long, but very striking kurta pyjama.

"It's good to see you," the man salaamed. "It's been a while. Chai?"

Mansingh nodded and they sat down on the floor amidst the array of colourful rolls of fabrics that were stacked floor to ceiling. A chai wallah arrived and dexterously poured three small cups of sweet chai tea that Indy received gratefully. A conversation on shirt fabrics began, the man with the kohl-rimmed eyes gesturing to an assistant to bring various bundles down for Mansingh to examine, three of which he eventually chose and, with a nod, was told to expect them stitched and ready to be worn by the end of the week.

Mansingh turned to Indy "And for you? We can find a ladies tailor to make whatever you want."

Her eyes widened and she hesitated for a moment, then shook her head. "It's all beautiful, but I think I am overwhelmed just now," and added, "Another time."

He shrugged and said his farewells, the palms of his hands touching in response to the salaam and they walked outside.

"You didn't like the fabrics?" he asked her, looking disappointed.

Indy put her hand to his arm reassuringly and answered, "I loved them! But I have no idea what I would like them to be transformed into. It's not the way we do things in Scotland." She laughed.

"You've got to give me a heads up if I am going to be a fashion designer, you know." Mansingh thought for a moment and then said seriously, "You can't leave Ahmedabad without some hand block fabric. Ahmedabad is famous for its fabrics – it was known as the Manchester of India in its day. Hand block, Bhandani tie-dye, mirror work." He looked at her baffled expression and grinned, shaking his head. "No problem, you are right. Take your time; we still have the Mirror Market to visit still, maybe that will tempt you."

"*Phew!*" She laughed. "I could do with a break and a sit down. How about some lunch?"

He nodded and they walked out of the market towards a group of rickshaws waiting outside the huge stone gates.

"Gopi Dining Hall," he informed the driver and turned to Indy with a grin. "I hope you're hungry."

Mansingh and Indy were led into a large room, filled with diners, the waiters weaving between the tables carrying huge trays, stopping regularly to refill bowls and deliver food. They took turns to visit the hand wash station and returned to their table, where immediately a large platter arrived in front of them, each with five small bowls, complete with a tall metal cup in which buttermilk was poured.

"This will be good for you, it will ease the heat from the chilli," Mansingh explained.

Indy smiled. "You forget, my mother is Gujarati. I may not have had a typical Indian upbringing, but the food at home was spicy and hot."

"So, you have been to a thali restaurant before?" he enquired.

She shook her head and saw a pleased expression cross his face. He was obviously trying hard to please her, she thought with satisfaction.

"So, it's like an 'all you can eat'. The waiters will keep coming around with refills till you have had enough to eat. The food is very fresh and very delicious. I hope you like it!"

She felt her stomach rumble and laughed. "It sounds great! I'm sure I will."

Mansingh smiled. "Do you want to have the sweet too?"

Indy nodded enthusiastically. "I'm in for the full deal."

The waiters served tirelessly, bringing a variety of savoury pastries, and ladling different sabjis and curries into the small dishes, with hot, soft rotis delivered efficiently with tongs onto the centre of the dish. There was no cutlery and she watched Mansingh's technique for scooping up the food with his fingers carefully. No sooner had she finished a bowl, then it was replenished. The sabjis were breathtakingly hot and slightly sweet – Gujarati style – and she realised that her mother had adapted their home cooking for Scottish tastes, reducing the amount of chilli enormously. The buttermilk was a welcome respite as was the accompanying sweet that was eaten alongside and at the same time as the rest of the food. A waiter arrived ready to fill the bowls again and she shook her head, placing her left hand on her stomach.

"No, thank you. I really don't think I can fit in any more."

He signalled to another waiter, who arrived with a huge tray of rice onto which a thin daal was ladled. Indy's jaw dropped and Mansingh roared with laughter.

"This is how we finish the meal." He laughed as she gathered her will power to scoop up the rice and daal with her fingers, groaning in her attempt to expand her stomach even further. They emerged into the heat and Indy clutched her belly. "That was amazing, but I don't think I will ever need to eat again."

Mansingh turned towards her. "So now what would you like to do?"

Indy groaned and answered, "If I were in Spain, I would say it's siesta time."

He shrugged, opening his arms wide to indicate that there was nothing he could do about that.

"Weren't you given a key to that woman's flat? Do you want help finding it? We could go there now."

Indy nodded, and they climbed into a rickshaw and headed to the address, her fingers wrapped around the key that she had placed carefully in the pocket of her handbag.

The flat was in another ubiquitous concrete block. One looked just like another to Indy and she was glad that Mansingh was able to help her interpret the address that was, like so many in India 'behind this, to the right of that' and would have been so much harder to locate if she had been on her own. As it was, it still took the driver a couple of stops while he conferred with other rickshaw drivers, making a few u-turns before finally arriving at the correct destination.

The apartment was on the second floor with a choice of lift or stairs, neither of them particularly inviting. Mansingh led Indy into the lift and pressed the button to ascend, allowing her to exit first, then gesturing towards the flat door. She brought out the key and gingerly turned it, half expecting it not to work, and felt the barrel turn over smoothly under the twist of her fingers, releasing the door that opened with ease before her.

The flat was small, consisting of a living room, small kitchen, bathroom with squat toilet and shower, and a bedroom. Arundhati had furnished it simply, but had obviously put some thought into the decor, the contents of which reflected the numerous countries she had visited. A batik hanging of a Balinese dancer graced the bedroom wall at the head of the double bed that was covered with a Rajasthani bedspread and by the side of the bed there was a rug that looked like it came from somewhere in Africa. It had obviously been a while since anyone had entered the room, as the tiled floor was covered with a layer of the fine dust that relentlessly pervaded Ahmedabad and she could see the footprints of her sandals as she walked. Indy moved from the bedroom to the living room and noticed that the furniture in both rooms was simple and contemporary. The living room had various cushions that looked like each one could tell its own story of origin; Mexican, Peruvian, Indonesian, and decorating the walls, shelves and surfaces were memorabilia, knick-knacks, statues and pictures from around the world. The rug in this room looked South American. Indy was surprised at how lived-in the flat looked, but then why wouldn't it be? It was, after all, Arundhati's home.

"Are you looking for something particular?" Mansingh's voice shook her out of her reverie.

She frowned in thought. "I'm not sure," she replied. "I'll just have a look around if you don't mind."

"Of course, but if you gave me an idea of what you might hope to find then I could look with you."

She pursed her lips in thought, and then shrugged helplessly. "I honestly don't know... maybe nothing, maybe something... I won't know until I see it."

Mansingh nodded.

Indy entered each room, and systematically opened every drawer and cupboard rifling through Arundhati's belongings. She had left Mansingh in the living room where he patiently settled himself into the sofa to wait and she counted her blessings that he had magically arrived into her life at this time, making her trip and these investigative forays so much easier and more fun.

Indy returned to the bedroom and opened the drawer to the side table next to the bed. Her fingers drifted across a packet of condoms, a box that contained a vibrator, then reached an unsealed envelope which she opened carefully, pulling out some photographs. An attractive young woman was pictured under palm trees, a cocktail in her hand, a wide smile revealing white teeth within red lips. She flipped to the next photograph that showed the same woman standing next to Prakash, their heads pressed together as she reached out her arm to take a selfie. Indy placed the photo into her bag and returned her gaze to the next photograph. It was of a large man standing by a pool, a gold chain around his neck and hair sprouting above the open shirt. She stared at it and pondered, then placed it in her bag with the other one.

Closing the drawer, she moved onto the chest of drawers. The top one had the usual pants and bras. *Does everyone have their underwear in the top drawer?* she mused as her hands rummaged the contents. Her fingers felt something solid and she pulled out an envelope, this one thicker than the one she had just investigated. She lifted the flap and gasped as she saw the contents. It was stuffed full of cash.

"Anything of interest?" She jumped as she heard Mansingh's voice behind her. He was standing in the doorway and she wondered if he had seen what she held in her hands as she swiftly placed it into her bag. She closed the drawer with some force and replied in a level tone, "It's hard to say." She turned to him with an apologetic smile. "Sorry to keep you waiting, I'll be done soon."

Mansingh remained standing in the doorway watching as she quickly ran her hands through the contents of the rest of the cabinet, finding nothing of interest.

"Just the living room to go," she muttered as she manoeuvred past him.

He lifted a laptop that he held in his hands and she looked at him with surprise. "I found this," he said, then added, "What did you find?"

Indy answered evasively, "Not much really." She stared at the laptop. "I wonder how we can access the password…"

"I could probably help you. Working at NID, there are lots of clever people there who might know how to get into it. If you like, I could take it and give it a try?"

Indy nodded. She plunged her hand into her shoulder bag, her fingers wrapping around Arundhati's phone and opened her mouth to suggest that he take that too, but suddenly remembered that she hadn't told him about Antwerp and released her grip. This would be something for her to deal with on her own.

"I think we've finished here," she said. *"Chalo jayie!* Let's go!"

Chapter 21
Ahmedabad 2018

It was another hot day in Ahmedabad. Question: What's the weather like today? Answer: The same as it was yesterday. Question: What will the weather be like tomorrow? Answer: The same as it was today.

Indy smiled at her private joke. Perhaps you had to be British to think it was remotely funny. You had to have lived on an island that produces four seasons of weather in one day and is always the main topic of conversation. *Careful,* she thought, *you'll be getting nostalgic.*

She was meeting Priya at Natarani Cafe.

"Take a rickshaw to Usmanpura, off Ashram Rd. Let's meet there for lunch –12.30?"

The driver pulled up outside a red brick wall, and she entered through a red brick archway behind and around which were a surprising number of trees, creating a green and shaded environment. It was a welcome relief from the concrete buildings and relentless sun that scorched so much of this huge city of Ahmedabad. The outdoor cafe had bench seats and tables designed to mould into the surroundings in sensuous curves, the light glinting on the mirror mosaics embedded into the surfaces, the sun's rays weaving through the foliage. It was quiet in the cafe and Indy chose one of the smaller booth-style tables to sit and wait for Priya. It wasn't long before she arrived, bike helmet in hand. Ordering two pudina lemon drinks from the counter, she sat down next to Indy and smiled.

"Are you enjoying Ahmedabad?" she asked.

Indy nodded. "I'm beginning to get the feel of it, I think. It's huge! I come from a country of five million people, you know."

Priya looked puzzled.

"In Scotland, that is," Indy explained, "so India is full on. But I love it," she added hastily. "And this place is really nicely designed."

Priya smiled broadly. "I thought you might like it. This is the home of Darpana, a dance theatre company. It has a theatre at the back and classes in dance and yoga so if you stay for a while, it could be useful for you to know about. I'm sorry," she hesitated, "I didn't recognise you before at the airport. You are Detective Inspector McKinley."

Indy rolled her eyes. "Please don't apologise! I'm here on holiday." She laughed. "Well, I'm meant to be here on holiday, anyway. Do you mind me asking you some more questions about Arundhati?" She pulled out the photos from her bag and handed them over to Priya who took them carefully in her hands. She gazed at the photograph of Prakash and her friend and a tear rolled down her cheek.

"It's Arundhati and Prakash. They look so happy." She wiped the tear away with an apology. "I can't believe she's gone." Priya gently moved the photograph behind the next one and jerked backwards with surprise.

Indy looked at her. "What is it?"

"It's Ajay Bhatwedekar," she replied, her voice in a whisper.

Indy leaned forward, with a questioning expression, as two glasses of pudina lemon arrived in front of them. They drank thirstily, enjoying the fresh lemon mint drink, and Priya looked

145

at Indy.

"He's a businessman who flies regularly with us. He was quite…" she paused to choose the right words before continuing, "quite flirtatious with Arundhati. I spoke to her about it early on, but she just laughed. I knew she enjoyed the attention, but she was having an affair with Prakash…"

Indy nodded.

Priya continued, "Prakash's wife was pregnant, but it didn't stop her. I didn't approve and it wasn't my business really."

"So why did you concern yourself about Arundhati and Ajay?" Indy asked.

Priya took a while to reply. "I don't know. She was in a relationship with Prakash and he was a married man. I told her that was stupid, but it had been going on for a long time and I suppose I had got used to it. It was almost like they were a couple. I'm not sure why Ajay's interest in Arundhati bothered me…Perhaps I didn't like to see her being unfaithful to Prakash!" She laughed. "Silly, I know." She returned her eyes to Ajay's photograph. "But why would she have his photograph?"

Indy looked at Priya. "So, Arundhati never mentioned she was seeing Ajay?" she asked.

Priya shook her head. "No. But to be honest, I saw less and less of her over the last two years."

Indy tilted her head, encouraging Priya to continue.

"I don't know why. Arundhati always seemed to be busy." She shrugged. "Maybe I should have asked her about what was going on in her life, but I didn't."

Indy smiled sympathetically. "These things happen. What does Ajay do for a living?" she asked.

"I think he's a property developer."

"You said he flies with you regularly. What are his

146

destinations?"

Priya thought for a minute. "He flies to Johannesburg, Harare, Gujarat, Goa, Dubai and recently Antwerp."

Indy thought for a minute. "Antwerp?" She furrowed her brow, trying to make a connection between the destinations. "Harare is an interesting destination for a property developer, isn't it?"

Priya shrugged in response.

"When did Ajay begin to fly to Antwerp?"

"Earlier this year. He went quite regularly, I think, with occasional visits afterwards."

Two menus were placed in front of them and they took a minute to consider their orders that included a couple more pudina lemon drinks. Despite the shade, it was another hot day in Ahmedabad.

"Do you think Arundhati could have been having an affair with Ajay?" Indy asked.

Priya took a minute to consider. "It's possible. Maybe that is why I saw less of her – she would have known I would disapprove. But why would anyone want to murder her?" she entreated.

Indy bit her lip. She had no wish to implicate Prakash, even though she could place him at the hotel where Arundhati was killed, having seen him there with her own eyes, and the possibility that she was having an affair with Ajay made it increasingly plausible that he was the murderer. The inevitable jealousy of a ménage à trois.

She shook her head and answered sincerely, "That's exactly what I plan to find out." Putting Arundhati to one side, they ate their lunch, enjoying getting to know each other better, after which Priya took Indy to show her Natarani Amphitheatre. A tall dark-haired young man approached them, greeting the two of them with an enquiring gaze. Priya immediately introduced themselves, adding that Indy was a well-known actress from the UK.

The man nodded, informing her that he had starred in many Gujarati films. "You are Anglo-Indian, aren't you?" he enquired of Indy.

"My mother is from Gujarat – from Ahmedabad, actually. My father is Scottish."

He smiled. "So you have family here."

Indy's face gave little away as she replied, "I don't know them, and I don't know where they live. They didn't approve of the marriage."

The man looked sympathetic and then said, "Family is important, but you can make your own. Come, let me show you around."

He took them on a guided tour, explaining that the signs of building work were due to Natarani Theatre having lost land at the bottom of the amphitheatre that used to lead straight down to the river.

"We used to be able to see the river and look straight across to the other side," he said regretfully.

"Now there is a walkway along the river and a road that makes a lot of traffic noise, disturbing our performances. We have had to build a soundproof wall, but I think the architecture is beautiful, don't you?" he said, gesturing to the interesting design that juxtaposed the bricks like building blocks, staggering length and width in turn. Leading them down past the amphitheatre, he showed them the new museum that was in the process of being constructed and was dedicated to the famous dancer Mrinalini Sarabhai who established Darpana and was instrumental in bringing Bharatanatyam classical Indian dance from South India to the north.

"I hope to see you again," he said with a winning smile as Priya and Indy thanked him.

"The woman who runs Darpana is very famous, Indy," Priya whispered, then added with a giggle, "Almost as famous as you, perhaps. Maybe next time you will meet her."

Indy laughed.

They walked out of the gateway that was reminiscent of a temple, towards Priya's motorbike.

"Can I give you a lift anywhere?" she asked.

Indy's thoughts drifted to Mansingh and the laptop. "Do you know a college called NID?"

Priya chuckled. "Of course. Hop on."

Indy manoeuvred her leg over the seat behind Priya and then remembered, "I don't have a helmet," she said.

"The passenger doesn't need one," Priya replied as she revved the engine and slid forwards. Indy clung onto the metal back of her seat as Priya weaved in and out of traffic fluidly.

Everything about the journey seemed treacherous and Indy was full of admiration for her new friend's motorbike skills.

Arriving at a building that was more modern in design than she had expected, she removed herself gingerly from the motorbike and thanked Priya as well as her lucky stars for delivering her to her destination safely. She was excited about surprising Mansingh and finding out what luck he had had with the laptop and then suddenly, she remembered Arundhati's mobile phone that still nestled in her bag.

"Priya, do you remember Arundhati's birthday?"

Priya nodded and answered, "Of course, it was 4 May 1990."

Indy smiled. It was too easy, but then again, in episode 5,

Death by Desire, a vital clue had been down to accessing a phone using the killer's personal information. The writers had done their research and discovered that most people used birthdays or memorable dates such as anniversaries for their keycodes. It was worth a try.

"Indy?" Priya hesitated. "I don't know if it is important, but the last time I saw Arundhati was at Mumbai airport when she was about to fly to Antwerp. She handed me a small package and asked me to post it. It was for Prakash."

Indy considered the information. "And did you?" Priya looked confused at the question. "Post the package?"

Priya looked surprised. "Yes, of course."

Indy nodded and waved, turning to walk towards NID. Students were everywhere, and she was directed inside the building to a woman who looked up at her over her reading glasses from her desk.

She introduced herself and asked for Mansingh Desai.

The woman looked at her doubtfully and shook her head. "Which department does he work in?" she asked wearily, as though she had many, far more important things to get on with.

Indy paused, realising with horror she had absolutely no idea.

The woman sighed, looked at the crestfallen face opposite her, took pity and typed his name into her computer. Scanning the screen, and scrolling down, her head tipped back to peer through the lenses of her glasses. She finally turned to Indy with a serious expression.

"There is no Mansingh registered here. I have checked and double-checked. Perhaps you have come to the wrong college?" She stared at Indy who turned away perplexed, thanking her for her troubles as she walked away.

If she were at home, this would have definitely been an occasion to get herself a drink, but being in Ahmedabad, a totally dry state, it would have to be an alcohol-free beverage. She settled into a nearby cafe and ordered herself a cold mocha, pulling out Arundhati's phone. The battery was flat, of course, but the same make as her own mobile. Looking around for a socket, she plugged her charger into the phone, aware that it could take a while. Hell, she had nothing better to do, she reckoned.

She pulled out her mobile and scrolled to Mansingh's name, pressing the handset icon. After a few rings, she heard his voice answer with a warm tone, "Indy."

"Hi, Mansingh, where are you?"

He replied without hesitation, "I'm with the IT guys trying to crack the password for the laptop. What about you? Are you having a good day? I'm sorry I haven't been able to show you around."

Indy's lips tightened as she replied, "I went to see you at NID, but you weren't there. In fact, the woman at the desk told me you weren't even listed on the computer."

There was a silence on the other end of the phone long enough for Indy to wish to break it. "Mansingh? Did you hear what I said?"

"I heard you, Indy. What are you accusing me of – lying? I work for the IT department that services NID, I'm not surprised they haven't heard of me. There are a lot of people who work at the college. Technically, I suppose I could have told you that I work for a company that works for NID, but I didn't think I needed to go into the small print with you." His voice was cold and distant on the other end of the line.

Indy closed her eyes as he spoke, cursing her lack of faith.

This was the man who had been so helpful and generous towards her. She could kick herself for questioning him – what reason had he for lying to her?

"I'm sorry, Mansingh. It was just a surprise and she looked at me as though I was an idiot. Perhaps I am. Will you forgive me?"

"Of course," he answered, the lightness returning to his voice. "Did you find out anything of interest from Arundhati's friend?"

"Maybe," she replied enthusiastically in her desire to restore his confidence in her. "I found a photograph of Arundhati with a man when I was looking through her things in the bedroom, and showed it to Priya. She recognised him as Ajay..." She rummaged through the notepad on which she had written his name. "Ajay Bhatwedekar, a wealthy property developer. It looks like they might have been having an affair, possibly for quite a long time. Priya says they met in 2015," she added.

"Ajay Bhatwedekar? I have heard of him. He's a very wealthy Ahmedabadian," he answered smoothly. "Three years is quite a long affair," he mused.

They finished the conversation arranging to meet the next day, and Mansingh's last words hung in the air. According to Priya, Arundhati had met Ajay in 2015, and had seen less and less of Priya socially since then. This was not a brief fling. So why had Arundhati not confided in her friend? Why had Priya still thought that Arundhati was having an affair with Prakash? Arundhati had had no problem sharing the fact that she was having an affair with a married man whose wife was pregnant, so why the secrecy regarding Ajay?

She opened her phone and googled Ajay Bhatwedekar, searching through the images. There were plenty of photographs of him at public events, but none with Arundhati. She googled his profile. A very wealthy man indeed, with photographs of the hotels and businesses he had in South Africa, India, and the United Arab Emirates. Recalling the destinations that Priya had mentioned, she searched for any sign of him owning property in Zimbabwe, but found nothing, so why would he be travelling there? She clicked her fingernails on the table and looked at the percentage of charge on Arundhati's phone. This was going to take a while, and there was a limit to how many coffees she could drink in succession, so she packed up the phone and charger and headed back to her hotel.

Three hours later, she held the mobile in her hands and closing her eyes while she made a silent wish for success, she keyed in 040590. She let out a whoop of success as the screensaver revealed a photograph of a colourful flower rangoli arrangement. Indy swiped to the camera icon and scrolled through the images. Various selfies appeared: in her uniform with the crew, relaxed and casual in jeans or shorts, glamorous in figure-hugging dresses, looking more traditional in Indian kurtas and sarees, posing sexily in a swimsuit by a beautiful pool, all with exotic backdrops in locations around the world. Not to mention the ubiquitous photographs of plates of food. There were a very few pictures of her and Ajay, and scrolling further back there were a few photos of her and Prakash.

Indy re-scrolled through the photographs again. It surprised her that there were so few of the man Arundhati had been having an affair with for three years. She closed her eyes in thought. Why would that be? Double-checking google, she confirmed that he wasn't married, but something made her sure that the relationship must be illicit.

She swiped to the WhatsApp messages and a broad smile

153

appeared on her face. Arundhati may have been circumspect in her photography, but not in her verbal communication or in her deletion of messages. It appeared that Prakash showed increasing frustration at Arundhati's unavailability and her regular excuses that she was working a lot on long haul flights. However, her exchanges with Ajay were very enthusiastic, with quite suggestive descriptions of what she would like to do to her lover if they could only be together – messages that received mostly emoji responses. It seemed Ajay did not spend much time on his replies. Indy scrolled on. There were arrangements made to meet up in Goa where it seemed he had a house. Presumably a pool too, Indy mused, remembering the photographs. There were also texts arranging to meet up at hotels, the names of which were familiar from the research Indy had done on Ajay and the property he owned. Indy scrolled through more texts between Arundhati and a person simply named JC. She paused for thought, noticing that there were no words used in these exchanges, only emojis, repetitions of the same symbols arranged in different sequences; thumbs up, international flags, planes taking off and landing, bullseye target, slice of cake and a selection of faces with different expressions. She checked the flags to identify the countries they represented: South Africa, India, Zimbabwe and Belgium. Re-scrolling the texts, she saw that the Zimbabwean flag had stopped being used around the time that the Belgian appeared. Why was that? She leaned back in her chair and sighed, trying to make sense of it all.

It would be interesting to find out what Mansingh had discovered on Arundhati's laptop tomorrow. She was looking forward to exchanging information with him.

Chapter 22
Calicut 2018

Sonal sat on her bed twisting a gold locket between her fingers. Her face was drawn and tired, the result of several sleepless nights. The fury of finding her own locket in his flat in the drawer of his bedside table – the gold locket that Prakash had given her for her 24th birthday, with a note asking him to keep it safe for her until they next met, proving that he had given the locket to that woman Arundhati – had long since dissipated. The fury had been supplanted by pure fear.

Sonal had gone to Prakash's flat in Mumbai knowing that both he and Indy had left for Antwerp. She rarely visited Prakash's home away from home, and it wasn't until she had met Indy that she realised that she had settled into a state of acceptance in her marriage. She had accepted that they lived with his domineering mother. She had accepted that he spent most of his time away from her. She had accepted that he was probably having an affair. But it was time for that to change.

Mumbai 2018

Arriving at the door of the apartment, the spare key to Prakash's flat liberated from the drawer in his bedside table in her handbag, Sonal felt every nerve end in her body quiver, alert to the danger of being caught in the act of trespass.

She pulled out the key, slotting it into the keyhole with caution, almost as though she half expected Prakash to be inside.

155

The key turned with ease and the door opened.

Sonal's gaze assessed the decor. It was basic and functional and without any personality. She sighed at the thought of how much she had always wanted to decorate her own home; a place for her, Prakash and their son. She wandered through the small flat that comprised a living room, a bedroom, a bathroom and a small kitchen and wondered how much time he spent in this soulless place. She gritted her teeth, reminding herself of why she had come.

She wanted – she needed – to find evidence of his affair with Arundhati to put her mind at rest one way or another.

A fire of resolve ignited and she moved with intent, opening drawers and cupboards, rifling through folders and boxes on the shelves. She growled as she came across a small scrapbook, obviously put together by Arundhati, that contained photographs of her and Prakash, punctuated with snippets of love messages and memories dating back years.

Without realising what she was doing, her hands tore the pages apart, scattering them on the bedroom floor. She reeled round, enraged, pulling the drawers out, upturning them, the contents tumbling around her feet. She kicked them savagely and turned to the bed. Her eyes took in the bedside table and she laughed mirthlessly as she saw it had a small drawer. Prakash kept everything of importance in the drawer of his bedside table at home. She wrenched it out and sobbed as she saw her gold locket inside. She reached down to pick it up, the memory of him giving it to her burned into her mind. She had seen it in the window of a jewellery shop and had pointed it out to him. It was coming up to her birthday and much to her surprise and joy, he had gone back later and bought it for her, giving her a kiss as he fastened the clasp around her neck, complimenting her on how beautiful it looked on her. What was it doing here? A piece of paper lay in the drawer underneath where the locket had been and she unfolded it. It was from Arundhati asking him to keep her locket safe – *her* locket! – until they saw each other again. A primal scream of rage emanated from her body as she tore up the note, her fingers taking a vicious pleasure in ripping the paper into tiny pieces before scattering them to the air. How dare he! How could he have given that woman her locket?

Sonal felt the fire within her body erupt like a volcano as she swept through the rest of the flat, upturning everything that stood in her way, before finally, spent and exhausted from her anger, she burst into tears and collapsed in a crumpled heap onto the floor.

Calicut 2018

Sonal dreaded returning to Prakash's family home. She felt her mother-in-law awaiting like a spider in heat, judging her, willing her to fail so that she could keep Prakash to herself, mothering him, smothering him, forever tied to her umbilical cord.

Sonal had fought for her position in Prakash's life and had failed. She hadn't replaced his mother, and he had replaced her with another woman. Arundhati. The anger within her had subsided for now, replaced by sadness at her loss. The hopes and dreams of a happy marriage filled with joy and children had disintegrated into an insignificant pile of unwanted tasteless crumbs.

She entered the large hall of the house that had rarely felt like home and quietly removed her sandals, softly crossing to the stairs, passing the door to the living room where no doubt her mother-in-law would be watching the latest drama unfold on her favourite TV soap opera. Entering her bedroom, she closed the door and collapsed onto her bed, her hand reaching for the locket that she had placed around her neck. Her fingers closed around it firmly and she wrenched the chain, breaking it and then throwing the locket across the room. It flew into her dressing table, smashing against it and landed on the floor. Small shiny jewels skittled along the polished surface and Sonal stared at them in surprise. She moved towards them, picking them up and placing them in the palm of her hand, then reached down for the locket. She had always known that the locket had opened, but had never kept anything inside it, although she had often thought that she should have photos printed of Prakash and her son, or a lock of their hair. She held one of the gems up to the light and gasped at its luminescence. It looked like a diamond – but how could that be?

Placing them back inside the locket, she scanned the room for a safe hiding place, before finally burying it amongst her underwear in the top drawer of her chest of drawers.

Calicut 2018

Prakash eased himself carefully out of the taxi, wincing with every movement. The x-rays at the hospital had shown his arm to be broken, and his shoulder socket dislocated. It had needed to be reset and he now wore a sling and had a support wrap around his chest due to a broken rib. He had extensive bruising on his body, his face, around his jaw and left eye. He dragged his suitcase with some difficulty from the cab to his front door, pausing before he entered. Prakash had tried to prepare a believable story for his state of appearance, but his head ached and the path through his fogged brain was dim and unclear. He couldn't think of any reason for him to turn up at home after a business trip looking the way he did.

Sonal was descending the staircase as he kicked off his shoes and she let out a shriek at the sight of him. The shriek acted like an alarm bell for Prakash's mother who flung open the living room door, her whole being primed to probe the latest drama. She caught sight of Prakash and screamed, running towards him with her arms outstretched as he backed away in fear of the potential pain this could incur.

"What happened to you?" She gasped as Sonal stood watching in silence from the stairs. "Come, come, sit down. Shall I get Dr Rajgopal to see you? Was it a car accident? Why didn't you let us know?"

Prakash gently eased his mother away from him, his eyes meeting Sonal's. Her gaze was implacable, and he moved past his mother towards her.

"Are you all right?" she asked him without emotion.

He tilted his head to one side in a non-committal way and turned to his mother. "Can I have a coffee?"

Swiftly, she jumped to the mission, rushing into the kitchen to give the order.

Sonal looked at him. "What happened, Prakash?"

He bit his lip, his eyes darting towards the kitchen to check his mother was out of earshot and answered in a low voice, "Burglars ransacked my apartment and beat me up. I think it's best my mother doesn't know."

Sonal stared at him, puzzled. "But…" She paused. The last thing she wanted him to know was that she had been the destroyer. He looked at her, surprised that she looked confused instead of shocked and she asked, "Why would they beat you up?"

Prakash shrugged. "I have no idea. The flat was a mess and they kept asking me where the diamonds were. I have no idea what they were talking about, but they dragged me out and kept beating me to get me to tell them. I tried to get them to understand I know nothing about diamonds, but they wouldn't listen." Tears filled his eyes as he relived the experience and Sonal ran her hand over his oiled hair as a mother would to a child.

She had frozen momentarily at his mention of the diamonds and chills ran through her. She struggled not to tell him that she had these jewels, these dangerous, desirable, beautiful jewels upstairs in their bedroom, tucked away in her drawer. She would have to confess that she had sneaked into his flat and done her utmost to destroy it. It was best he didn't know. He had been through enough and karma had ensured that he had paid the price for his adulterous affair. He must never know that she had searched his apartment. A sudden realisation that these men could have entered when she was there caused her stomach to flip in fear. Supposing they had seen her leave? No, that wasn't possible. If they had, they wouldn't have attacked Prakash. She had an urgent desire to rid herself of the diamonds quickly. Their presence in the house felt like a beacon attracting danger like a signal of doom. But what should she do with them?

She would phone Indy, Indy would know what to do.

Chapter 23
Ahmedabad 2017

Arundhati swung lazily in the hammock under the shade of two mango trees. A gentle breeze caressed her skin as she enjoyed the rhythm of the rocking movement that soothed and relaxed her like a baby. Her mother had often told her that they used to place her in a makeshift hammock made from a length of cloth and tie it between two trees, the rhythm of the swing gently rocking her to sleep as her parents enjoyed their picnic.

A shadow passed over her and she opened her eyes to see Ajay's large frame standing over her. He was scowling.

"Trouble?" she asked, worried that her visit to this Goan paradise would be ruined by his bad mood.

He snorted angrily and she manoeuvred herself out of the hammock, lowering her feet to the ground to stand near him.

"Let me get you a drink and you can tell me all about it," she said, gently placing her hand on his arm and leading him to a lounger. She signalled to a manservant to bring him a whisky and settled next to him.

"What's happened?"

He ground his teeth, spitting out the words. "Bloody Modis, both of them."

She raised her eyebrows waiting for him to continue.

"As if demonetisation wasn't enough to ruin my business." He threw out his arms, looking directly into her face. "Who the hell thinks that getting rid of cash is a good idea? It will be the end of India!"

Arundhati nodded in agreement. Who could miss the hardship demonetisation was causing. As a flight attendant, she constantly had to deal with travellers who were unprepared for not being able to use their bank cards in machines because the ATMs had run out of cash, or if they were lucky enough to find a machine with money in it, there was a strict limit as to how much could be drawn. People had become alert to which bank machine was active, which ones had been refilled with cash and they would swarm like bees, waiting hours for a few rupees. Tourists, normally dripping with cash, ready to spend it bountifully on stalls, wandered past helplessly apologising to the street market sellers who were unable to bring home enough to eat that day. Ironically, Modi said he was demonetising in order to catch crooks dealing in the black market and therefore able to avoid paying tax, but it was the poorer people as always who were suffering. Wheeler dealers like Ajay could always find a way around – it was little more than an irritant for someone like him.

"Who's the other Modi?" she asked.

"*Ha!* Bloody Nirav Modi, no relation to the other idiot." He growled at the thought. "As if it isn't enough that I have had to put up with not being able to access cash, now Nirav Modi, the bright shining face of diamonds, is being investigated for fraud. Word is that he's involved in defrauding the Punjab National Bank. It could cost billions of rupees."

Arundhati gasped. "Nirav Modi? The diamond designer? The man who has all the famous actresses wearing his jewellery?"

Ajay chortled. "Yes, the bloody jewellery designer. I could kill him."

162

Arundhati struggled to grasp the importance of the fraud and looked at him quizzically. He sighed.

"This fraud affects Surat in our very own Gujarat, where I have been getting the diamonds cut and polished. It seems Modi's been using units to divert diamonds worth billions to domestic markets illegally. Things are tightening up and" – he chortled mirthlessly – "I can't afford my diamonds to be looked into too closely." He looked at her, wondering how much she knew about how his business worked. She had never enquired and they had never discussed where his diamonds came from, or the technicalities of getting the diamonds from source to delivery, beyond her own not invaluable input. Her lack of inquisitiveness suited him well, but now he felt the need to talk about it, if only to work through the implications this disruption might mean to his organisation.

"Look," he began and continued as though explaining his information to a child, "I get my diamonds from mines in the Cameroons which, as I am sure you know, is right next to the Central African Republic. Mining is a tricky business," he hesitated, "there's a lot of red tape involved which I like to avoid. A few years ago, something called the Kimberley Process was brought in, supposedly to prevent exploitation of miners – working conditions and all that – but to be honest, it just makes life difficult for people like me." Ajay was pleased to see Arundhati's look of sympathy and forged ahead. "You see, it's very easy to get around the Kimberley Process. All diamonds need a certificate to say that they are mined fairly, but how do I know what is fair and what isn't? That's none of my business. The world's corrupt and you might as well get the most out of it." He leaned towards her and cupped her chin affectionately, a smile stretching across his face. "Don't you agree, my sexy courier?"

She grinned, nodding in response, pleased Ajay was sounding more relaxed. It boded well for her visit.

"It's very easy to get Kimberley Process officials to certify diamonds to say they are conflict free." He chuckled, warming to the subject. "You can even get them to help evade airport taxes – for the right price. I get most of my diamonds from Gbitti because it sits right across a narrow stretch of river separating it from the Central African Republic. The diamonds from Gbitti look the same as diamonds from just across the river where they come under the Kimberley jurisdiction."

Ajay saw her puzzled look. "You thought all diamonds looked the same?"

She nodded as he let out a belting laugh. "Most people do," he continued, "but people in the know can tell where diamonds come from; they have different colours amongst other tell-tale signs. Anyway, it's so easy to get from the Cameroons to Central Africa; there's a stretch of river between the two countries with wooden canoes that pull you across on a steel rope. Crazy, eh? That's Africa for you!" He rolled his eyes. "Corruption is everywhere. Zimbabwe is just as bad. I've dabbled with importing diamonds from there, but I've decided it's not worth it. The Kimberley Process thinks they can sort out diamond mining in that country, but they can't. Soldiers just set up their own syndicates and run the mines, and the diamonds are certified and exported as Kimberley ones and conflict free." He waggled his head as though considering the unjustness of the state of affairs before turning to Arundhati again. "*Ha!* What a business, *eh?*"

There was a silence as Ajay's face darkened again, remembering why he had started this one-sided conversation. "It's all been so easy till now. Collect the diamonds in Cameroon, get them to South Africa, transport them to India – thanks to you, my dear – and an easy trip to Surat to get them cut and polished. But I'm worried now that Surat is too hot. I will have to take my diamonds elsewhere."

She nodded thoughtfully. "Is there anywhere else in India?" she asked. Ajay shook his head angrily. "No. I will have to look at Antwerp."

Arundhati looked up in surprise. "Antwerp, Belgium?"

He grunted, "Yes." Waggling his head, he realised his mood had lifted. "But I have you, my dear. What's the difference between you taking them from South Africa to Belgium instead of India? Anything is possible, right?"

Arundhati returned his smile. She wondered how indispensable she was to him. Perhaps, the time was coming to find out.

Chapter 24
Ahmedabad 2018

Indy lay in bed staring at the hotel room ceiling. She had treated herself to a refurbished Haveli Hotel in the old part of Ahmedabad and if the rest of the unrestored buildings in the neighbourhood were anything to go by, the hotel had been rescued just in time. The building was beautifully designed and the restoration paid close attention to detail, making the most of the superb original craftsmanship. An inner courtyard was designed to circulate the air and keep the interior cool without air conditioning, and was a place where guests could enjoy peacefully, swinging in a traditional hanging wooden sofa, adorned with colourful cushions, their minds soothed by the gentle sound of water from a fountain nearby. Indy's bedroom was tastefully decorated and she loved it.

Lying in a carved wooden bed, under a delicately hand-embroidered bedspread, her head supported by an array of cushions, she marvelled at the huge wooden beams that reached from one side of the ceiling to the other. This hotel was her treat, her luxurious nod to being on holiday – a concept she was determined to cling on to, despite the feeling that the 'holiday' aspect was not exactly what she had planned.

The conversation with Priya was playing like a looped re-run round and round in her mind. What had she learned of significance from the information? She was sure that Ajay was a key to this puzzle, but how? She mentally repeated the destinations Priya had mentioned; Johannesburg, Harare, Gujarat, Goa, Dubai and Antwerp.

What was the link between them? Why would a property developer build in Harare? Surely under Mugabe's regime, Zimbabwe was not the most obvious choice for investment? And was the package that Arundhati had given to Priya of importance?

Her eyes followed the beams down the wall to a colourful hanging with small round mirror pieces stitched in. They sparkled in the sunlight that streamed through the long window, sending spots of dazzling reflective light cascading across the walls like jewels.

Indy sat bolt upright and threw the top sheet to one side. *The Hidden Casket*, episode 65, sprung to mind. How had it taken her so long to see the similarities? In *The Hidden Casket*, the storyline told about gems smuggled out of India in a casket to a Scottish Castle during the Raj. There they were hidden in an attic, only found during building refurbishments. The gems had ostensibly brought bad luck to all those involved, including to the person who found them in the attic, who was found dead which was where Detective Inspector McKinley had come in to solve the case.

Indy grabbed her phone and quickly put in a search for 'diamonds'. Several articles with information about blood diamonds popped up and she exhaled audibly. Could the package Priya had posted to Prakash have contained diamonds?

She typed in Sonal's name and pressed call. "Indy?"

Indy was relieved that Sonal's voice sounded pleased to hear from her. "I've been meaning to call you."

"How are you, Sonal? How is Prakash?"

There was silence on the other end of the phone.

"Sonal? Is everything all right?"

"He's getting better, but he's still in a lot of pain. Indy, I found something and I don't know what to do."

Indy couldn't help herself. "Did you find diamonds, Sonal?" She heard Sonal gasp.

"How did you know?"

Indy grinned. "Well, you were the one who insisted I was a detective. Tell me about it, Sonal." She listened while Sonal recounted how she had found the diamonds and was terrified because she realised that they were the cause of Prakash's assault and that they were both in danger.

"I don't want them, Indy. I don't care how much they are worth. Can you get them back to whoever owns them and tell them we are sorry. Please!" She begged.

"Send them to me, Sonal." she soothed. "I will do what I can and you can trust me not to mention your name to anyone."

She gave Sonal the address of the hotel in which she was staying and then asked, "Has Prakash mentioned anything about his trip to Antwerp?"

She could almost hear Sonal's brain ticking over as she considered her reply. "He doesn't talk to me about his business, Indy."

"Sonal, I think you know what I am talking about. Arundhati was killed in Antwerp."

Sonal's reply sounded indignant and desperate. "Prakash had nothing to do with that. He didn't go to Antwerp – he was in Mumbai. He may be many things, Indy, but I can tell you he is not a murderer. Surely you are not suggesting…?" Her sentence remained unfinished, the potential reality hanging in the air like mist.

"I am not suggesting anything, Sonal." Indy's manner was calm and soothing. "I am just asking you if he has mentioned anything, or if you had asked him about it."

There was a long pause while Sonal collected herself enough to answer in a choked voice, "We will not talk about that woman again. She has gone and I am glad of it."

Indy was left holding the phone, but Sonal had gone.

Fifteen minutes later, Mansingh arrived at the hotel dressed in jeans, sandals and a hand block printed shirt. It was crisp and freshly ironed, the outer edge of the sleeves looked like they could cut through butter like a knife. Indy had learned that no self-respecting Indian either male or female would go out in clothes that hadn't been properly laundered. And this included ironing. An 'istri wallah' was worth his or her weight in gold.

She smiled. "Is that one of your new shirts?" she asked.

He nodded, looking pleased that she had noticed.

"It's beautiful," she complimented him.

He had the laptop under his arm and held it out to her. She received it, looking at him questioningly.

"It's unlocked," he answered.

"You didn't find anything of interest in it?" she asked.

Mansingh waggled his head. "It's not my business," he replied, "I wouldn't know what to look for."

She nodded. "I'll take it upstairs… Would you like to see my room?"

They climbed the stairs to the second floor, admiring the view down to the courtyard as they rose higher, overlooking where they had been standing below. Her bedroom was light and airy in feel. From the large window at one end, there was a bird's eye view of the narrow streets of the old city of Ahmedabad.

"It's amazing," Mansingh told her, "that so much of this area is still ruinous, dilapidated and falling to pieces. But some people have recognised the beauty and value of the architecture. These buildings are perfectly designed to capture air, cooling the interiors naturally. And that isn't the only amazing thing about them – the artisanship is fantastic. Look at the detail of the wood carvings used in the lintels, doors, beams and support columns. A couple of decades ago, you could pick these items up for nothing in salvage because nobody valued the buildings in the 'pols' or alleyways as you might say. The streets are small and narrow so not really suited to cars; although, of course, the locals still live here, but none of their houses have been improved. Maybe the renovation of these buildings will make people look at the neighbourhood with more respect." He chuckled ruefully. "Although, if that happens, I suppose the locals will be priced out of their homes." He looked around the room with satisfaction. "They've certainly done a good job." He turned to look at her. "*Acha*, we are going out, *yar*? Where shall we go today?"

Indy shrugged her shoulders.

Mansingh lifted his index finger authoritatively, and proclaimed, "Kankaria Lake, Gujarat's oldest and second largest lake, and a sort of leisure park. *Calo!*" And swinging his arm to gesture a forward action, Mansingh directed her out of the room.

Kankaria Lake turned out to be very large indeed. Seventy-six acres of artificial water to be precise and a focal point for an amusement park and hot air balloon rides, yoga, joggers and gentle strolls. Indy and Mansingh settled down on a bench with an ice cream to watch the Ahmedabadi enjoying leisure time.

At last, Indy could contain herself no longer and turned to Mansingh with enthusiasm, recounting her findings on Arundhati's phone, her conversation with Priya, and her belief that Ajay and Arundhati had not only been having an affair but that Ajay was a diamond smuggler. She hesitated as she

170

suggested another thought that she had been having. "I was wondering if Arundhati could have actually been the carrier for the diamonds. I thought I would ask Priya if it is feasible for her to have been smuggling them between countries. I mean, they're small, aren't they, so perhaps she could manage it quite easily." She paused before she admitted to him, "I found something else in her flat that I didn't tell you about at the time."

Mansingh raised his eyebrows in query.

"A wadge of money in her drawer. And Priya said she had seen Arundhati's handbag with a stash of money too. If she was involved, then that could explain her having so much cash."

"I think there's something else you didn't tell me you found," he said with a smile. Indy looked at him in surprise, unsure as to what he was referring.

"The phone. You must have found that in the flat?"

Indy paled, realising that she hadn't told Mansingh that she had seen Prakash in Antwerp. She nodded, "um, yes. I don't know why I didn't mention it."

He laughed gently and reached for her hand, "You've done a lot of work, Indy, I'm impressed. But what can you prove?"

She bit her lip in thought.

"Let me think about it, Mansingh. I feel sure I am on the right track, but you are right, I need more proof." She smiled at him. "Thanks for listening. I'm sorry if this is boring for you, I feel like I'm obsessing and it's taking over my life! But I can't help it. Now that I've come so far, I want the answers to what's happened – to me, to Prakash, and to Arundhati herself." She rose from the bench as if to signal the end of the conversation.

"Come, let's see some more of the park, isn't that what we are here for?"

They wandered along the lake, enjoying being away from

the traffic chaos of the city.

"This park is particularly beautiful at night when everything is lit and Kankaria looks magical," Mansingh told her. He paused momentarily, then asked, "Are you going to see your family while you are here?"

Indy took a sharp intake of breath, surprised at the suddenness of the question. "Honestly, I'm not sure, Mansingh. My mother gave me their address if I wanted to get in touch, but I don't know. I can't believe they cut their own daughter out of their lives for marrying my father. I'm not sure if I want to see them."

They walked on in silence and Mansingh said softly, "Seeing you might be just what is needed to heal the relationship."

She felt herself drawn into his dark brown eyes and the dark brown lashes that framed them. Why was it that men so often had the thick lashes that women so desired? Her eyes scanned his long aquiline nose, admiring the sculptural features of his face, and her fingers reached towards him, touching his arm lightly. Her body moved towards his imperceptibly.

"You're a good man, Mansingh," she whispered.

Their eyes locked, the two bodies a hair's breadth apart as they absorbed each other, then the moment passed as he moved away.

Chapter 25
Mumbai 2018

Ajay was on his 25th lap, letting off steam like the Drop of Doom in an amusement park. Business was doing well since his move to Antwerp, and the slight hiccup of the missing diamonds had not caused any undue repercussions. He heaved himself out of the pool, signalling for a towel which was produced within seconds and proceeded to pat himself dry before settling into a lounger. He was looking forward to meeting with Mansingh this morning and hearing what progress he was making with tracing the missing diamonds. He didn't like loose ends, but time had brought perspective, and he had to take into consideration that Mansingh might be better employed elsewhere if this undercover investigation with Indy Monroe was fruitless. He had been short-changed some diamonds, but on the other hand Arundhati was dead, so in some ways perhaps the debt had been paid.

His thoughts were interrupted by the announcement of Mansingh's arrival and he raised himself to a seated position to welcome him with a firm handshake. If there was one person Ajay felt he could trust, it was Mansingh. He owed his life to this man who had proven his loyalty by stepping in front of Ajay and taking the bullet meant for him. It had been a close call for Mansingh who had swung his body sideways so that the bullet had miraculously only grazed his arm, causing a minor wound. Mansingh had retaliated swiftly, chasing after the men who turned and ran like the cowards they were. Ajay was eternally grateful to him.

He couldn't understand why they had been unexpectedly cornered by a couple of police officers. It was something that should not happen. Ajay paid a lot of money for protection from the police force in order for him to carry out his lucrative business without interference. How they had known where he was and why they pulled their guns on him was something he had brought up forcefully with the police chief who was happy enough to take his money in return for turning a blind eye.

Which was what Ajay made sure he got in return.

Clicking his fingers to signal for coffee for himself and a chai for Mansingh, he gestured to him to sit.

"How are things, Mansingh?"

Mansingh shook his head in thought. "I found Arundhati's laptop," he stated flatly. Ajay's frame stiffened.

"I managed to access it and I erased any links to you so you have nothing to worry about on that score."

"Where is it now?" Ajay asked.

"I returned it to Indy. She was with me when I found it so I thought this would allay any suspicions. I told her there was nothing of interest in it. She trusts me." He grinned.

"Good. But I wonder if there is any point in continuing with this actress woman. She clearly knows nothing, and you are too valuable to be wasted on a pointless task – however pleasurable it is for you," Ajay added with a smile.

Mansingh removed his sunglasses and twirled them thoughtfully in his fingers.

"She's dogged, Ajaybhai, and she's becoming interested in you. I think for the moment it is a good idea I keep an eye on her so she doesn't ask inappropriate questions to the wrong people."

Ajay furrowed his thick eyebrows. "Perhaps we should get

rid of her," he growled.

Mansingh stopped twirling the glasses and placed them back on his face. "I think that is a last resort if you don't mind me saying, Ajaybhai. Her death would attract unwanted publicity."

Ajay frowned and then said, "Are there any other leads? Arundhati had a friend who was also a flight attendant. What was her name...?"

Mansingh looked at him. "Priya," he answered.

"Yes, Priya, that's the one. Do you think she knows anything? They were very good friends and you know what women are like. They like to gossip."

Mansingh nodded his head thoughtfully. "From what I can tell, Arundhati was smart. I doubt she would have said anything about her involvement in your business even to her friend." He looked up at Ajay. "But I am happy to check Priya out if you like."

Ajay briefly considered the suggestion then shook his head. "No, I don't want your cover blown. You focus on this actress. I'll get someone else to check out Priya." He smiled suddenly and said brightly, "So, Indy is interested in me? Excellent. I think I could have a bit of fun with her myself." He chuckled. "I've got a super idea. Bring her to the Arts for All sponsorship party next week and I will introduce myself."

Mansingh looked at Ajay with surprise. "Ajaybhai, how would I explain getting an invitation?"

"I will send you an invitation as a member of staff at NID. NID college is one of the institutions I support. I support quite a few charitable causes." He chuckled. "It's important to be seen to do the right thing." Pausing a moment for Mansingh to acknowledge his little joke, he added, "I leave it in your capable hands as to how you get her to come, but I am sure you can manage it. I look forward to meeting her."

Mansingh nodded thoughtfully. "Of course." He rose from his seat and said, "I am really glad I was able to talk this over with you. I knew you would have good advice for me."

Ajay leaned back in his lounger with a satisfied smile. "No problem, Mansingh," he said. He was looking forward to meeting this woman.

Ahmedabad 2018

"Six p.m. at the Mirror Market. Perfect," Indy said. "I'm looking forward to seeing you, Priya." She was genuinely excited about the prospect of visiting a night-time market and seeing her friend.

But before then, she was meeting up with Mansingh at Gandhi Ashram followed by lunch. Something else to look forward to.

She stepped out of the hotel into the pols, the narrow lanes of the heritage city, enjoying strolling past the crumbling buildings. She was constantly amazed that people lived in these once-beautiful old buildings, for so many of them looked in danger of being condemned. As she passed, a woman dressed in a sari, the end of the length of fabric pulled over her hair, smiled and waved at her and she smiled back. There seemed to be no ill will towards her and Indy felt safe walking through the streets. It contrasted starkly with how she felt walking through certain neighbourhoods in Scotland. She doubted very much that they would be exchanging friendly greetings, or perhaps any greeting at all.

It was a long walk to Gandhi Ashram from Old Ahmedabad and she wasn't planning on walking the whole way. Ahmedabad was hot, dry and dusty, and once onto the main roads, the traffic was noisy and chaotic, but at home Indy was used to walking and for lack of any other exercise, she had decided to try to keep the habit up as much as possible.

She turned the corner, arriving at one of the many pol junctions; this one opening up to a beautifully ornate well in the centre. A cow slowly strolled past, a sight that Indy had become accustomed to in India and it always made her smile. She paused to look at one of the many beautifully carved wooden doors and became aware of a man hovering at the corner of one of the lanes behind her. Instinctively, she drew her bag close to her body and walked on swiftly, turning into another lane, cursing that it was small and surprisingly empty, a rare feat in such a busy city. Quickening her pace, she weaved towards the left into another alleyway, her ears alert to the sound of footsteps behind, and at the end of the lane she turned swiftly to see if he had followed. He was there. Her heart beat fast as she debated her options. Rapidly picking up the pace, she was relieved to turn the corner and find herself in a bustling street with a well-attended chai stall and a small market with fruit and vegetable stands. She made straight for the chai stall, ordering a cup and sat down on a chair offered to her with a nod by the chai wallah. The man wearing dark glasses and a green T-shirt paused momentarily before strolling by slowly without acknowledging her presence. She watched him as he passed and noticed he had a large tattoo of a tiger on his forearm.

A small cup of milky sweetly spiced tea was handed to her and she received it gratefully. Indy pulled out her phone to check where she was. Walking was all very well but at this moment, it felt safer to catch a rickshaw to her destination. That way, she had a chance of shaking him off if he was tailing her, and if he wasn't, then she could breathe a sigh of relief anyway.

Taking her last sip of chai, she handed the cup back to the

chai wallah with thanks and walked towards two auto rickshaws who were parked by the side of the road. She negotiated her destination with the driver at the front and stepped in, turning her head to check behind her as it drove off. Tiger man was standing there, and when he caught her eye, an imperceptible smile flickered across his lips.

Mansingh was waiting for her outside Gandhi Ashram. Gandhi had moved back to Ahmedabad on his return from South Africa, setting up his ashram that grew rapidly in popularity, with land on which to farm. His return had been instrumental in giving an important boost to the mill workers at a key time in their demand for a fair wage from the textile mills and it was from this ashram that Gandhi had led the famous Salt March in protest at the unfair tax on salt in 1930. He had begun his third fast here, a fast that lasted three days, proving the strength of his beliefs in satyagraha, the non-violent resistance that inspired his followers. Indy walked around the compound that housed a handicrafts centre, a handmade paper factory and a spinning wheel factory, plus two new permanent exhibition galleries on Gandhi's life that had opened at the ashram just the year before. It was a reflective Indy who settled herself down under a tree outside Gandhi's home.

Mansingh stood beside her, leaning against the tree trunk. "You like the ashram?" he asked.

Indy closed her eyes, and remained silent, then shook her head as if to sift through her thoughts.

"Like?" she answered softly. "I'm in awe of somebody like Gandhi. Somebody who will face the threat of injury and death with no violent resistance. People think they are brave when they have a weapon in their hands. They are cheered and admired, but how much braver are those who face down violence without that weapon."

Mansingh took a moment to reply. "It doesn't always work though, does it? If your family were being threatened, what would you do?"

Indy frowned. "I would fight with everything I have."

He chuckled. "So…?"

She nodded in response, searching for clarity. "The instinct to protect is powerful and in that moment when someone I love is threatened, I hope I would find the strength to fight and not freeze with fear. But what Gandhi represents is the bigger picture. He doesn't advocate non-violence out of fear. He participates fully and is willing to stand in front of aggressors to show them he is strong and will look them in the face. He is saying that violence is not the answer."

"But, sometimes," Mansingh said, "it is the only answer people understand."

They walked out of the gates onto Ashram Road in silence. The sun felt relentlessly hot, the dust rising from their sandals as they moved into the noise.

"God I'd love a beer," Indy said.

Mansingh laughed. "Well, you can blame Gandhi for our dry state. You'll have to make do with fresh juice or buttermilk and a delicious lunch. How about going to a restaurant that is in the Guinness Book of Records for making a 4ft dosa, the longest dosa in the world?"

Indy smiled. "Sounds perfect." She laughed. "But I think I'll order a smaller one."

She paused as she looked back at the ashram. "It makes me proud to be Gujarati, you know. Maybe that seems silly to you. But there's a part of me that has never fully belonged. I am

Scottish, but not fully Scottish; Indian, but ignorant of India. When I decided to come to India, I wasn't being honest with myself. I told myself it was for a holiday. But I know now, I have come to realise, that I chose to come to India to find out about the half of me that has been like an empty vessel waiting to be filled with first-hand knowledge and information of real life and real people – not just from books and films – so that I can feel Indian, not just be Indian. Coming here is nothing like reading about Gandhi or watching the film. This brings it to life and makes me legitimate."

Mansingh looked at her inquiringly. "Your parents aren't married?" he asked, sounding surprised.

She laughed. "No! I mean, yes… that isn't what I meant. Yes, they are married, though actually I am not sure my father believes in marriage, but it was important for my mother. Not only is it what she would have expected, but marriage legalises the relationship and it would have been necessary for her immigrant status, especially for an Indian."

"There's racism in Scotland?"

Indy shrugged. "There's racism everywhere, isn't there?" she answered. They signalled for a rickshaw and Indy stepped inside.

The man with the tiger tattoo was smoking a cigarette and standing on the opposite side of the street, watching.

Chapter 26
Ahmedabad 2018

It was a hot March in Ahmedabad this year and even at six p.m. the temperature was 36C. Indy smiled at the thought of how her friends and family in Scotland would react in this heat. The average Summer in Scotland was between 15–17C and on those rare occasions when the temperature rose above 20C, people who had spent all year complaining about the cold, the wind and the rain would start complaining that it was too hot. Indy felt a sudden, unexpected wave of nostalgia for the British preoccupation with the weather, that no one who didn't live on an island would understand. She knew the frustration of waking up to sunshine, then finding yourself drenched with rain two hours later. She understood the complexity of trying to pack economically for a Scottish summer holiday that requires clothes suitable for cold, wet, sun and rain. She looked out of her hotel window into the darkness. Here, it was so predictable. Dark fell at six p.m., and she knew that she would wake up to sunshine and it would be hot or hotter. She longed to be surprised. Grinning at her fickleness, she shook her head at the human capacity for dissatisfaction. She should count herself lucky she could afford a hotel room where air conditioning meant it was a constant 22C.

She had arranged to meet Priya at six thirty p.m. and as she emerged from the hotel into the heat, her eyes scanned the dark street for her stalker. This time, she had arranged in advance for a rickshaw to collect her from the hotel and take her to her destination. It was strange, she reflected, how vulnerable the dark could make one feel. It whittled away confidence.

Priya had enjoyed a day off and had spent it helping her mother make preparations for her niece's birthday. The child was the first grandchild to be born, and was now ten years old and her grandmother doted on her. Priya came second in a family of four children, and was the oldest of the two sisters. Both her brothers were married with five children between them and lived in the family home much to her mother's approval and satisfaction. Priya's younger sister Seema hadn't married yet, but she didn't think it would be long, as things seemed to be moving forwards with Seema and Manu and both sets of parents were in agreement that an arrangement should be formalised soon. Priya's parents had not given up on matchmaking Priya, but much to their frustration – and Priya's relief – her work took her away from Ahmedabad for unreasonable amounts of time, making it difficult for her mother to arrange meetings with suitable men. It wasn't that Priya didn't want to get married, but she wasn't willing to give up her freedom just yet, especially if it meant moving in with a mother-in-law.

Thankfully, the birthday celebration was in the afternoon, leaving her free to meet Indy at the Mirror Market for six thirty p.m. Her mother had been keen for Priya to invite Indy to the birthday party, but Priya felt sure that Indy must have better things to do and made excuses for not asking her.

"Who wouldn't want to come to a party and meet your family?" her mother had asked, gesticulating into the air with outstretched fingers.

"Ma, you make it sound like we are getting married. She's from the UK. They don't do family things in the same way."

"What do you mean they don't do family things? They have families, don't they? They celebrate birthdays, don't they? It's a party. She might like to see how we do parties in India. Ask her," she ordered before turning on her heels, indicating the end of the conversation.

Priya sighed and reached for her phone. Against her better judgement, she typed in Indy's number and pressed call.

"Hello, Indy? We are still meeting at the Mirror Market this evening, *yar*?"

"Of course, Priya, I'm looking forward to it," Indy answered.

"Super. It's just that my mother has asked if you want to join us for my niece's birthday party this afternoon. I'm sure you have better things to do, Indy, so don't worry about saying no."

Indy let out a disappointed sigh. "Oh, Priya, I would have loved to, but I'm going to Gandhi Ashram this afternoon with Mansingh. Please thank your mother for the invitation. It's very kind of her."

"No problem, Indy. I thought you would have made plans already. See you six thirty, yes?"

"Six thirty, Priya. And thanks again for the invite."

Priya walked through to the kitchen calling her mother, "Ma! I asked Indy, but she can't come. She says to say thank you."

Her mother was up to her elbows in flour, kneading dough with the palm of one hand and wiping a floury finger across her brow with the other hand to shift a hair back into place. She grunted, shaking her head. "There is nothing more important than family, Priya." She looked up from her work, raising her voice to be heard. "Do you hear me? Where would we be without family? Nowhere, that's where." Clicking her tongue between her teeth, she turned back to her kneading, calling out once more, "*Calo*, we've got work to do."

Climbing astride her scooter, Priya headed out to the Law Garden where the Mirror Market was based. It was not often that she got the opportunity to show friends around her city and she was excited to play tour guide to Indy. The Mirror Market was a perfect showcase at night time; the mirrors stitched into the traditional Gujarati fabrics dazzled and reflected in the artificial light. Stalls were filled with goods, selling everything from hangings, cushions, and clothes to small stuffed toy camels. The animals' graceful lolloping gait was a rare sight in Ahmedabad now, but still a common enough one in the rest of Gujarat where they were used in much the same way as work horses once were in Scotland.

She had arrived a little early, glad of the opportunity to escape from the family. It had been a lovely party, but she had become used to her own space, a privilege of which Indian families were sometimes blissfully or perhaps deliberately unaware. Parking her bike, she was about to remove her helmet when she sensed the presence of two men standing close to her, one on either side. They each reached an arm around her waist, crossing her from behind and trapping her between the bike and their arms so that she couldn't turn. She felt her stomach drop, turning her legs to jelly, and tried to scream, but nothing came out.

"Priya, isn't it?" the big man said. "What a lovely name."

They led her away from the market. It was dark and no one took any notice of the group of three walking towards the gardens. Turning into a group of trees, they pressed her against one of the trunks, the big man smiling, displaying brown and red stains on irregular teeth. Priya had had time to recover from the shock and found her voice, "What do you want?" she whispered. "I'll scream if you don't let me go."

A large hand reached around her throat, encasing her neck with ease. "I wouldn't do that if I were you. We want to ask you a few questions, so just listen and answer us and there'll be no need for any screaming." He turned to look at his friend, the man with the thin face, "Will there?"

His friend chuckled, waggling his head from side to side with a grin. "So," the big man continued, "you were a friend of Arundhati, yes?" Priya's eyes widened with surprise as she nodded in reply.

"*Acha,*" the big man seemed pleased with her response. "So what do you know about her business?"

Priya glanced from one man to the other with a confused expression.

"She was a flight attendant?" she replied hesitantly, aware that they must know this, but unsure what the correct answer was. She could feel her phone buzzing in her pocket and remembered she had put it on silent during the party, something she had got used to doing for her work.

The man's hand tightened slightly, just enough to cause her some discomfort.

"Don't take us for fools, Priya. I said, what do you know about her *business*?" He emphasised the word 'business' as though it had a special meaning.

Priya gasped and he relaxed the squeeze.

"What kind of business do you mean? I'm not sure what it is you want to know…" she whispered huskily.

"Tell us about her personal life," intercepted the thin man in a high, reedy voice. The big man looked at him in surprise and he shrugged. "Well, I think you needed to be more specific," he said in response to the big man's gaze.

"She was having an affair with a married man," Priya said.

185

She racked her brains wondering if there was anything else she could possibly say that would be of use. Her phone vibrated again and she knew it was probably Indy wondering where she was.

"*Hmm,*" the big man grunted, "did she tell you anything else?"

The thin man stepped closer, his hand moving to lift her top. "Perhaps this will help you remember," he slid his hand upwards towards her breast. He could feel her quivering with fear, trying to push him away and he began to salivate. He caught sight of the big man looking at him out of the corner of his eyes.

"What? The boss never said we had to take care with this one, did he?" He licked his lips having reached her breast.

Priya squeezed her eyelids closed, her body trembling with fear and disgust. She heard a sudden crash and felt hands releasing their hold from her neck and breast. Opening her eyes, she saw a man in a green top standing over the two thugs who lay on the ground at her feet. They were holding their heads, blood trickling between their fingers. He had a lathi in his hand and he wielded the bamboo stick high in the air, bringing it down with all his might over their heads and bodies. They moaned helplessly as he took a rope from his belt and proceeded to tie them up, binding them together, then gagging them with efficiency. Priya stared at him, speechless, rooted to the ground and then pulled her top down, feeling tears spring to her eyes.

The man in the green top glanced towards her, holding a hand out, palm upwards to show he was no threat and tilted his head to one side as though to ask if she was OK.

She nodded and slowly moved away from the scene, gathering speed as she left him behind. But not before she noticed he had a large tattoo of a tiger on his forearm.

186

Indy perused the market as she waited for Priya to arrive. Many of the stalls invited the shopper to enter the space, every inch of which was covered with attractively bright and colourful fabrics, the smiling man or woman keen to make a sale. She had learned not to engage with the sellers unless she was really interested as once an interaction started, it was almost impossible to get away. She didn't really understand how to barter, especially when asked what she was willing to pay for an item, a question calculated to baffle tourists who had no idea what the price should be. Priya had told her that bartering was half the fun of buying at the market, so Indy was looking forward to learning some techniques. She checked her watch. 6.35 p.m. Priya was only five minutes late. She double-checked the meeting point on her phone, and decided to call Priya, though she was aware that if she wasn't at the market yet, she would be on her scooter unable to take a call.

She continued walking, admiring the array of embroidered skirts shimmering with mirrors and smiled at the thought of wearing one back home. A beautiful dream but totally impractical.

"Ma'am? You like the skirt? Come," a young man, waving his hand, beckoned her to approach the stall.

She shook her head as he called after her. "Ma'am, only three thousand rupees... Ma'am!"

Indy shook her head and checked her phone again. 6.40 p.m. She felt a niggle of annoyance rise within her at having to wait and she scrolled to Priya, pressing call. No answer. Sighing heavily, she continued browsing the stalls, avoiding the eager man with the skirt, and her eye caught sight of an embroidered shoulder bag. It was time to commit to the evening, with or without Priya, she thought.

187

She fingered the bag, an action that resulted in an immediate response from the stall holder who eagerly pulled down as many bags as he could for her to see, complimenting her good taste on each and every one in which she showed any interest. Remembering that Sonal had told her to halve the price asked for, she followed this advice and bought the bag, the stall holder shaking his head vehemently at her bargaining skills and then smiling broadly at her as she walked away, eagerly holding out more items for her to buy.

It was 6.45 p.m. and there was still no sign of Priya. She retraced her steps to the meeting point, scanning the area then pressed call again, but received no answer. Her excitement in the Mirror Market had dissipated. Half the fun had been the prospect of meeting up with Priya, but she was reluctant to cut the evening short and head directly back to the hotel so she wandered over to the Khau Gallee food stalls. She ordered some bhajiyas and stood eating them, dipping them in spicy tomato chutney as she watched groups of families and friends passing by. It seemed that no one did anything on their own in India which made her feel lonely, isolated and slightly vulnerable. It was seven p.m. now and she had given up on Priya joining her.

Turning to discard her plate, her eyes caught sight of a man in a green top in the distance. She stiffened, searching to get a clearer view. Without giving it a second thought, she moved into the crowd to find him, weaving her way through the lively chattering groups competing with each other to be heard. She scanned from left to right but there was no sign of him and she stood feeling like a stranded whale with the sea of people flooding like waves around her. A man jolted her arm and she turned quickly, clutching her shoulder bag tightly as he hastened to apologise, moving on with a gesture of hand to heart. He was wearing a green top and she exhaled deeply. That man was nothing like the man with the tiger tattoo and she felt stupidly paranoid. It was time to get a grip on herself and enjoy the evening. She would engage with the shopkeepers, buy some presents and enjoy herself.

An hour later, she felt she had only seen half of what was on offer, but she was now carrying an assortment of bags filled with a variety of treasures. She stopped at a stall with the thought of buying a large bag in which to put all the small ones and glanced up at a tall mirror that was being used to reflect the image of a woman trying on an embroidered skirt. This time, there was no mistake. The man in the green top with the tiger tattoo on his arm was standing at the edge of the crowd, watching her. She moved away from the stall quickly, darting between the people, doubling back to lose him, her heart pounding. Coming to a stop, she looked around and felt a pang of fear that he was still there.

Episode 71, *The Mindful Murderer* came to her mind. In a market scene, similar to this, Detective Inspector McKinley was being followed so she tucked herself into a vennel and turned the tables on the killer by initiating a surprise attack. Her eyes darted from right to left, looking for an alternative to an alleyway. There was a gap between two stalls, so she ducked swiftly, manoeuvring through the shoppers and made her way towards it, keeping low so she could slip in without being noticed. The man passed just in front of her and stopped to scan the crowd. She could feel herself holding her breath, aware of the sound of her heart thumping. He reached for his phone and spoke to someone as he continued to spin slowly, obviously in search of her. He placed his phone back into the breast pocket of his shirt, and continued walking while Indy slowly crept forwards in pursuit. In episode 71, her key element of surprise before she did her highly proficient kung fu-like moves on the killer was a gun placed between his shoulder blades. Not exactly an original idea, but it had worked a treat. Indy rummaged around in her bag to see if she could find anything that would feel remotely like the end of a gun and felt her fingers wrapping around a flute that she had bought as a present. It would have to do. Taking it firmly in her fist, she moved towards the man, steeling herself for what was about to happen. The showdown. The fight. The climax of the story – McKinley against the villain yet again.

"Indy?" a friendly voice shouted her name loudly from behind.

She wheeled around to face Mansingh, her jaw open in surprise, her hand directing a flute towards him like a toy gun. Confused, she turned back towards the man in green, but he had gone. It was her turn to scan the crowd, but he was nowhere to be seen and she wheeled around again, annoyed and frustrated.

"What are you doing here?" she asked, her face and voice barely concealing her irritation.

Mansingh didn't rise to what sounded very much like a challenge. "Are you going to kill me with a flute?" He laughed.

Indy looked down at her hand and returned the flute to its bag. "What on earth were you doing?" Mansingh asked.

Furtively, she looked around her again, and furrowed her brow in thought as she wondered how her prey had disappeared so fast.

"I was being followed and it's not for the first time, so I decided to confront him and was just about to when you appeared."

Mansingh raised an eyebrow. "That sounds dangerous. Where is he?"

She looked at him and shrugged. "He's gone. He managed

to evaporate when you called my name. I don't know how he could have got away so quickly."

"Well, I'm glad he's gone. I thought you might be here, so I came on the off chance of finding you. And thank goodness I did. I don't like the idea of you challenging someone to a fight." He grinned. "But are you on your own?" he continued. "I thought you were meeting Priya."

Indy shook her head, "She hasn't shown up and she's not answering her phone. I don't know what's happened to her."

Mansingh looked down at Indy and then said lightly, "Well, it's her loss. Have you eaten?"

She smiled. "I had some bhajiyas, and to be honest, I don't feel like eating anything. I think I might just go back to the hotel."

He nodded and guided her out of the market towards a rickshaw. "I'll see you to the hotel," he said as they climbed inside.

"So, tell me really," Mansingh said leaning towards her conspiratorially, "what would you have done if I hadn't turned up?"

Indy shrugged. "I would have led him somewhere a bit quieter and then found out what he was doing following me," she answered. She saw the doubt in his expression. "I've got skills. I know I'm an actress, but I've had to do a lot of training in self-defence and martial arts and stuff to look convincing when I fight." She giggled and rolled her eyes. "I spend a lot of time fighting as detective inspector." Indy examined his face. "You don't believe me?"

Mansingh shook his head. "I just don't think you should put these skills to the test. At the end of the day, you have only been faking it, haven't you?"

Indy raised her eyebrows. "I tell you what," she retaliated, "when we get to the hotel, you can try me."

Mansingh couldn't mask his surprise.

"We'll have a fight," she persisted. "Or don't you fight?"

"I don't normally fight women," he answered.

Indy dismissed the comment with a wave. "May the best person win." She smiled.

They arrived at the hotel and she led him up to her room where she kicked off her shoes. Looking around, she started shifting some furniture to create space then tying her hair up in a band, she clapped her hands.

"Ready?" she asked eagerly.

Mansingh looked at her helplessly. "You are joking, right?"

Indy shook her head slowly from side to side and shifted her weight. "Are you ready?" she repeated.

He put his hands to his face and moved them slowly downwards in disbelief and then nodded.

She moved towards him and he grabbed at her, but she slipped through his arm and spun round. He grinned and she smiled back. He circled her and she mirrored the move, facing him, but he suddenly was behind her, his arm around her shoulders. Indy bent forward swiftly and threw him forcefully over her head so that he landed on the floor.

"You OK?" she asked.

Mansingh nodded, appearing to get up slowly, but turned quickly, throwing her backwards as his head came between her legs. Like lightening, her legs grabbed him and she did a corkscrew action that unbalanced him, then leaped up, landing on top of him as he fell.

"Gotcha," she said with a grin. "Still doubtful about my abilities?"

He gazed up at her with admiration. "I never doubted your

abilities," he said.

Her jaw dropped in mock outrage. "You did so!"

He placed his hands on her arms and pulled her towards him.

"In fact, I would be interested in learning more about your abilities." He chuckled, lifting his head to kiss her.

The touch of his warm lips on hers opened a floodgate of emotions in her and she found herself responding with enthusiasm. How long had it been since she had been intimate with a man, she wondered. She relaxed into his embrace, pressing her groin into his and feeling him harden in response. He rolled her over and their eyes met as he paused, giving her time to change her mind. She reached up and undid the belt buckle on his trousers.

"We'll be more comfortable with this out of the way," she commented lightly. He smiled and leaned down to kiss her again.

Indy closed her eyes. It had been far too long, she thought.

The man with the tiger tattoo sat in his chair looking at the text message that he had received. *'Be more careful. That was too close.'*

Chapter 27
Ahmedabad 2018

Indy woke slowly, enjoying the unusual experience of nestling in a man's arms. She had fallen asleep in Mansingh's embrace, and he was still wrapped around her, her back against his front in the classic spooning position that works so well in young relationships. She pressed her backside into his groin and felt him stir, giggling at her power. Mansingh's lips nibbled her shoulder and his hand moved down between her legs and she moaned as he entered her. Last night, they had taken all the time in the world over their love making, exploring and familiarising themselves with each other's bodies, pleasuring and accommodating one another until they both achieved satisfaction. This morning, they enjoyed the rough and tumble of fulfilling desire, trusting one another to be comfortable with that need.

When they had finished, they lay together side by side holding hands.

Indy felt herself smiling and said, "I feel like the cat who has eaten the cream."

Mansingh laughed. "I like that expression."

The hotel room phone rang and she reached across him to answer it. "Thank you. Can you bring it to my room, please?"

She looked down at him, her long dark hair brushing his face.

"I think I might have my first tangible piece of evidence," she said as she rolled out of bed, pulling on a light cotton dressing gown and grabbing some money.

There was a knock on the door and she opened it just enough to receive a package, handing the man a tip and thanking him.

Mansingh raised himself to a seated position against the pillows as he watched Indy return, clutching the package in her hands. It was hand stitched into cloth and she looked around her for something to cut the threads, diverting to the bathroom for her manicuring scissors.

"What is it?" he asked.

She looked up at him briefly as she cut open the cloth wrapping.

"Just wait and see," she responded.

Inside the outer cloth, there was a thick paper packet and within that a small box. Holding it with reverence on the palm of her hand, she lifted the lid, then raised the wadding to reveal...

"Diamonds!" Mansingh said with a gasp.

"Diamonds," Indy repeated looking at him with a smile.

They stared at the gems, then held them up to the light, turning them slowly between their fingers.

"Who sent them to you?" he asked. Indy shook her head.

"What are you going to do with them?" Mansingh questioned.

She looked at him. "I need to return them to their owner, so that no one else gets hurt. I believe his name is Ajay Bhatwedekar," she answered.

Mansingh grinned. "Well, I have an invitation to an Arts for All sponsorship party he is having at one of his hotels in Mumbai. How would you like to come with me?"

Indy looked momentarily puzzled. "How on earth did you get an invitation from Ajay?" she asked.

Mansingh waggled his head. "He is one of the NIT sponsors, so as a member of staff at the college, I get an annual invitation."

She absorbed the information and then leaned over to kiss

him. "That sounds perfect," she answered.

Ahmedabad 2018

Priya lay in bed unwilling to get up. She could hear her family talking loudly, as always at maximum volume as though they had been born without a dial adjustment control. One of her nieces was crying and her brother was calling for his wife to look after the child, then Priya's mother's voice could be heard shouting at her son to do something about his own child then (she imagined) picking her up, clucking and tutting until the little girl's sobs eased.

"Has anyone seen Priya?" her mother asked.

Priya buried her head under the sheet, curling up in a ball and heard heavy footsteps climbing the stairs and the door was flung open.

"Priya? What are you doing in bed? It's nearly nine thirty!" her mother stated in an outraged voice.

Priya groaned. "Ma, I'm not feeling well. I don't want to get up," and she rolled over, her back towards the plump figure of her mother who was standing hand on hip in the doorway. The woman moved closer, landing heavily on the bed beside her as a hand reached towards her forehead.

"*Pyaari,* not feeling well?" She tutted. "*Hmm…* there is no fever. I will get you something and you will feel fine very soon. Then you will get up and get dressed and you will feel even better."

Priya's mother was not a woman to pander to people lying around. She had raised four children and now had a husband, two sons, their wives and her grandchildren living at home and firmly believed that many hands make light work. She exited the bedroom with authority, returning shortly afterwards with a brown liquid for Priya to drink, nodding with satisfaction as Priya gulped it down. "I will see you downstairs soon and you will drink a cup of masala chai. That will be very good for you. I will make it nice and sweet."

Priya sighed. She picked up her phone and looked at the unanswered text messages from Indy. She hadn't contacted her since that unbearable experience last night. Those hands on her body... her fingers formed fists and her knees squeezed together at the thought of what might have been. Thank goodness the man with the tattoo had turned up when he did. She saw the two men, large and lewd, staring at her, their faces close to hers, and she desperately tried to dispel the images with a shake of her head. If that man hadn't arrived when he did...

She knew she would have to phone Indy, but just at the moment she had no idea what to say. She couldn't speak about the experience to anyone right now.

She lifted her legs out of bed and got herself washed and dressed mindlessly. She gave no consideration to what she put on her body, plaiting her hair without thought before descending the staircase for the cup of chai she knew she had to drink.

Her phone rang in her hand and she looked at it reluctantly.

"Priya," her mother's voice said despairingly, "answer your phone! What are you doing?" and she manoeuvred her daughter into a chair, placing the small cup with hot brown liquid in front of her.

Priya pressed the green button to answer the call, willing her mother to disappear, and was relieved to see that her mother seemed satisfied that Priya had done as she had been instructed and turned on her heels to return to the kitchen.

"Priya? Are you OK? I waited for you last night, but you didn't come."

Priya closed her eyes and bit her lip, unable to speak.

"Priya? Are you there?" Indy persisted.

Priya nodded. Her heart was pounding and she realised that she was clutching the phone in her hand tightly. She released the grip and as the phone fell to the ground, Indy's voice could be heard repeating Priya's name to the empty space. Her mother returned, waddling towards her daughter, clucking her tongue with exasperation as she picked it up off the floor.

"Hello? This is Priya's mother. Who is this?"

Indy answered and her mother continued, "I don't know what's wrong with Priya. She came back early last night, didn't eat her dinner and says she isn't feeling well. She doesn't have a fever, but she isn't herself."

"Can I talk to her?" Indy asked.

Priya's mother held the phone out to her daughter who stared at it, shaking her head wordlessly. Her mother sighed heavily and said, "I'm sorry, but she can't talk right now. She'll phone you back when she's feeling better."

She clicked off and stared at Priya.

"What is this?" she asked with concern in her voice. "What happened to you?"

Priya looked up at her mother's large dark kohl-rimmed eyes that were staring at her full of love and her own eyes filled with tears.

"Oh, Ma!" she said as she felt the well of emotion rise and overflow, erupting in sobs as the tension within her was released. "Oh, Ma! It was horrible," and she wrapped her arms around the broad waist, nestling into the soft warmth of her mother's body, and felt safe as she was rocked from side to side in a loving embrace.

Chapter 28
Ahmedabad 2018

Mansingh stood watching Ajay finish his 50th length. He emerged from the pool, his powerful shoulders cascading a torrent of water like a fountain over his large body. Opening his arms to receive the generous towel that was delivered by one of his manservants, he wrapped it around his body. Then he gestured for Mansingh to take a seat and rubbed the towel vigorously over himself, snapping his fingers as the towel dropped onto the ground. The manservant arrived swiftly with a fresh pair of shorts and Ajay lowered his wet swimming trunks, stepping out of them like a lord, the manservant at his feet to receive them, then offering the clean dry shorts for Ajay to step into. Ajay nodded to the man kneeling at his feet, then lifted the shorts before sinking into a sun lounger and reaching for his glasses from the adjacent side table. Mansingh felt he had just witnessed a regal ritual as he watched the manservant scurry away, clutching the wet item in his hand. He half expected the man to remove himself from Ajay's presence walking backwards and bowing in the old way.

"There is something I need you to take care of," Ajay said. Mansingh nodded in agreement.

"I sent Jitu and Vasant to deal with Arundhati's friend last night and they managed to bungle the job."

Mansingh raised his eyebrows with interest.

"They were beaten up, then bound and left in the Law Gardens by just one man. He had a tiger tattoo on his arm. I want you to find out who he is and who he is working for. Nobody threatens Ajay Bhatwedekar."

Mansingh looked serious. "You think it is a rival gang?"

Ajay shrugged. "Vijay 'Kale Aainkhen' Kapadia, has shown signs of trying to muscle into my patch, but he has never done anything as bold as this. Attacking my men like this is out of order and I can't afford to let it go."

Mansingh nodded. "I will see to it, Ajaybhai." He shifted forwards, leaning towards Ajay. "I have managed to get Indy to agree to come to the sponsorship party in Mumbai. I think this is a great idea of yours, boss. You can question her yourself much better than Jitu and Vasant. Sometimes, the subtle approach works best." He laughed softly and Ajay looked at him with a grin.

"So the subtle ways are working for you then?" he asked.

Mansingh waggled his head, and Ajay reached over to slap his arm affectionately, letting out a huge belly laugh.

"Don't say I don't look after you, *eh*?" Ajay smiled.

"Never, boss."

Mansingh rose from his seat. "I will find out who this man is and when I do, you can let me know how you want me to deal with him."

Ajay nodded and reached for a cigar. A man rushed over with the necessary tools to snip and light it as Mansingh slipped away. He crossed the marbled entrance hall and was shown out of the huge wooden front door with a bow by a man dressed in peacock blue. Mounting his motorbike, he revved the engine and drove away through the slowly opening electric gates and the chowkidar keeping a watchful eye on anyone exiting and entering Ajay's mansion.

He drove for a short while then pulled up at the kerbside,

reaching for his mobile.

A deep voice answered, "Yes?"

"Where are you?" Mansingh asked.

"She's having lunch at the Green House," came the answer.

"Nice," Mansingh said. "Your job is nearly done. It's getting too close for comfort after last night and I've been given the mission to track you down." He laughed. "Well done, by the way. It's about time those thugs got what they deserved. I'm on my way now so you'll see me soon." He rang off and headed out to meet Indy.

Indy sat at a table in the leafy shade of the Green Room, an outdoor cafe placed on the ground floor of MG Hotel, an upmarket place to stay with an even more upmarket rooftop restaurant that she hadn't tried yet. Perhaps, she would treat Mansingh one evening.

She was confused by Priya's refusal to speak to her this morning and worried about her new friend who, she thought, must really be feeling ill if she couldn't talk on the phone. Indy pulled out her mobile and scrolled through her contacts to find Priya's name, pressing to message. *'Sorry to hear you aren't well. Do you want me to visit?'* She paused, hesitating while she thought about what else to say. She needed to ask Priya if, theoretically, it would be fairly easy for a flight attendant to smuggle diamonds through security, but was aware this was a peculiar question to ask out of the blue. It would have been so much easier to drop it into conversation. She sighed and continued her text, *'I hope you don't mind me asking, but there is a possible storyline for my TV series that involves a flight attendant smuggling diamonds through security. Would this be quite easy to do?'* Indy re-read the text and nodded, then pressed send.

"Do you mind if I join you?"

Her heart leaped at the sound of his voice and she turned to see Mansingh standing behind her bench. He stepped over to sit beside her, and they pressed their shoulders and thighs together.

"I would love to give you a kiss, but it's not done in India, I'm afraid," he said. "We will have to wait."

The waiter arrived and they managed to detach themselves from each other with difficulty. Indy's phone vibrated on the table and she looked down to see a message from Priya.

Opening it, she smiled and looked at Mansingh.

"Priya says it would be easy for a flight attendant to smuggle diamonds through security."

He nodded. "So, what are your thoughts?"

She pondered. "I believe Ajay got Arundhati to smuggle diamonds and was having an affair with her. We know that Prakash was threatened by two men, probably the same ones who threatened me. I am sure they are working for Ajay because they were looking for the missing diamonds that I think Arundhati stole and sent to Prakash. I'm not sure why she sent them to him though and I am not sure whether he knew he had them. She had hidden them in the locket he had given her. Exactly how involved was Prakash in Arundhati's affairs – was he involved in the plan to steal the diamonds?"

Mansingh considered what she had just told him, then asked, "How can you link the diamonds to Ajay?"

Indy smiled. "You said we were invited to a sponsorship party at Ajay's hotel in Mumbai. This may sound far-fetched but as Detective Inspector McKinley in episode 23, *Walls Have Ears*, I needed a confession from the criminal so one of the characters wore a wire. It was surprisingly small and easy to hide – not like the ones in the old films. I was wondering if you could get hold of a wire like that for me? Perhaps from someone in your work?"

Mansingh stared at her. "Indy, you have no idea how dangerous that would be. To extract a confession from a man like Ajay? He would have you killed before you left the hotel."

Indy returned the stare, then she laughed lightly. "My goodness, Mansingh, anyone would think you know the man! I don't see that there's much danger. I've been invited as your guest and you are just an ordinary person who has got an invitation because you work at MIT. No one is going to worry about us."

"I was just thinking that if Ajay is who you think he is, then he could be very dangerous," Mansingh explained. "What happened to your plan of just returning the diamonds? That sounds much simpler. We get in, leave them somewhere they can be found by him and get out without anyone knowing."

Indy looked at him as though she was considering this and then said, "Well, yes. We could do that, but then he would get away with it, wouldn't he? He's dangerous, Mansingh – I don't know how dangerous, but if my knowledge of crime is anything to go by, I reckon he is responsible for torture and even murders. This way, with a wire, I could make sure he doesn't threaten anyone again."

Mansingh buried his face in his hands and nodded slowly.

"OK. I will get you a wire. The party is on Saturday so we have three days."

Indy grinned. "Great. I will book accommodation and flights. My treat. I take it we will be sharing a room?" she asked coyly.

He placed his hand on her thigh and stroked it in confirmation.

"*Mmmm,*" she moaned, "I think we need to get a room now."

Mansingh detached himself reluctantly and said, "I wish we could, but I have a few things to deal with before we go." He leaned over and pushed his fingers into her hair, cupping the back of her head. "I'll see you very soon," he whispered.

She watched him go and calling for the bill, she paid and left the Green Room. Flagging a rickshaw, she held out an address, written in Gujarati for the driver to read. He nodded and drove off into the dusty, busy mayhem of Ahmedabadi streets.

After a long drive, the rickshaw arrived at what looked like an attractive older neighbourhood and pulled alongside the kerb. Indy peered out of the open doorway of the rickshaw and then turned in wordless query back to the driver. He nodded, speaking to her enthusiastically in Gujarati, gesturing towards a house, hidden behind foliage. She paid him, adding a generous tip and stepped out onto the roadside.

She felt the gentle flutter of butterflies in her stomach as she walked towards the mustard yellow house that was hidden by the rampaging garden like buried treasure. Standing on the doorstep, she inhaled deeply, then rang the bell. An old woman in a saree answered the door and not for the first time, Indy wished her mother had persevered in teaching her daughter Gujarati. She remembered feeling different enough as a child in Morayshire, desperately wanting to fit in and be accepted as fully Scottish like the pale, blue-eyed children around her. She had hated her mother speaking to her in a foreign language and had resisted speaking it herself. Now she was tongue tied as she looked at this woman, only managing to say "Arya and Dinesh Gupta?"

The woman nodded her head and stood back to allow Indy to enter.

Indy slipped off her sandals and stepped onto the cool marble. The hall was shadowed as though the sun never entered it. The walls looked like they hadn't been painted in decades and the furniture was old and untouched by any design influence in the past fifty or more years. Indy felt as though she had entered a time capsule into a faded 1950s world.

The old woman shuffled down the corridor leaving Indy behind who stood rooted to the spot, rotating slowly while she examined the artefacts around her.

"*Shu hu tamne madad kari shaku?*" a woman's voice said behind her and she was struck by how much it sounded like her mother. She turned and saw a woman in kurta pyjamas and caught the change of expression as she looked at Indy's face.

"Is it you?" she whispered. "It's Indira, *Dadi.*"

At the word dadi, 'grandmother,' Arya let out a sob and held out her arms. Indy moved towards her, entering the soft warm embrace with tears in her eyes.

"I never thought I would see you. I never dared to hope," she said as she rocked Indy from side to side like the baby she had never held.

She led her granddaughter by the hand to the living room, sitting her down, cupping Indy's chin in the palm of her hand with vigour and then releasing her, her hands clasped in front of her body while she drank in the sight of the young woman. Then she flung her arms up in the air, waving to Indy to stay put as she bustled out of the room.

Indy stayed rooted to the seat, breathless with anticipation for five minutes that seemed like fifteen. Finally, her grandmother returned, this time with an upright, white-haired man.

"*Dada?*" Indy said.

Dinesh seemed to dissolve in front of her eyes as his shoulders crumpled and he staggered towards her. Indy rose from her seat to hug her grandfather, then hug her grandmother and then they all hugged each other while they cried for the lost forty years.

Chapter 29
Mumbai 2018

The Mumbai Palace Hotel, owned by one Ajay Bhatwedekar, was just one of the five star hotels in The Bhatwedekar portfolio. The building was a bustle of energy and efficiency as layers of hierarchy directed arrangements for the evening's party. A cascade of micro management was in place, with several imperious autocracies in descending levels of importance issuing authoritative directives to their teams of uniformed minions. Not only was this event worth several lakhs, but it was for Ajay Bhatwedekar and nobody could afford to make a mistake.

Ajay, however, was feeling quite relaxed. He was nowhere near the hotel yet, having recently been for his morning swim. He sat in his office with a beaming smile on his face as he stared at the photograph in his hand. Mansingh was good. Really good. Like the son he had never had.

He took one more look at the image of the man with the tiger tattoo, the face turned to one side as he lay on the ground in a pool of blood that seeped from the knife wound across his neck. The man's face was beaten, his hair matted with blood. Ajay turned the photograph over and read the words, *'A gift for you on your special day. My pleasure, M.'*

Ajay's smile spread across his face and his taut convex belly bobbed up and down as he chuckled. He was looking forward to giving Mansingh a pat on the back this evening and a special bonus for his excellent work.

Indy held up the dress for Mansingh to see.

"What do you think?" she asked. "Is this appropriate for the occasion?"

"I think I need to see it on you," he answered, leaning back in the hotel armchair, his feet propped up on the king-size bed.

Indy slipped off her cotton dress and stepped into peacock blue silk. She zipped up the side, bringing the contours of the dress close around her body, the fabric skimming over her curves, flowing closely over her breast and hips then falling softly to the ground. Mansingh gasped at the transformation.

"I've never seen you like that," he said.

Indy laughed. "Well, you needn't act so surprised," she teased. "I hope I don't have to wear a flimsy dress for you to be impressed by the way I look." She turned to the mirror, "Is it OK for this evening? It's not too... Revealing?" she asked.

Mansingh shook his head. "It's perfect. Take a dupatta with you and then you have something for your modesty if you feel the need, but I wouldn't worry. This party will be full of the rich and famous and they will be wearing the latest fashions, I am sure. I expect a lot of the women to be in very skimpy clothes." He laughed.

Indy chucked a pillow at him and placed a hand on her hip. "Well, don't get too excited." She laughed as she undid the dress and slipped it to the floor.

"Oh, I'm excited already," he said as he rose from his chair towards her, lifting her out of the pool of fabric as he carried her to the bed.

Indy and Mansingh stepped out of the hotel to be greeted by Sandeep who was grinning from ear to ear and clapping his

207

hands. With a waggle of the head so vigorous, it looked like it could detach itself and fly away, he exuded delight at the sight of the pair.

"I am driver to the stars," he said. "I can't believe how you look. You leave Mumbai and return looking like royalty. I am honoured to be your driver tonight." He held open the door to his Padmini with pride.

Indy and Mansingh smiled at Sandeep and then at each other and stepped carefully into the taxi.

"We should have hired a limousine," Mansingh whispered.

Indy elbowed him, shaking her head. "I couldn't not have Sandeep drive us. We may not be arriving in style, but we will be delivered with love."

Mansingh laughed. "Delivered with love. Well, that's a first," and he put his arm around her shoulders. Indy looked up and saw Sandeep smiling at them in the rear-view mirror. Of course, he wasn't looking at the road, she thought with a chuckle.

Arriving at the hotel, Mansingh took Indy's hand as she stepped out of the taxi. She took extra care as she lowered her head under the roof of the cab's doorway.

"Just call me, anytime, it doesn't matter how late. I will be there!" Sandeep shouted joyously. They waved to him and stood, looking at each other, preparing themselves to enter the hotel.

"Are you ready?" Mansingh asked, squeezing her hand.

Indy nodded and they moved towards the entrance and joined the queue of expensively dressed people in formal evening attire waiting to enter.

Security was strict. Mansingh had explained that since the Mumbai bombings of 2017, security had tightened even more than before so Indy was prepared for her bag and body to be screened. She beeped as she walked through the doorway and was led to one side. Indy felt her heart pound as the woman beckoned her into a curtained booth and asked her to remove her shoes then passed a wand over her body. Indy held her head up high, and laughed lightly. "It's probably my jewellery?" she suggested.

The woman finished scanning and nodded without saying a word, apparently satisfied and then waved her out. Indy exhaled deeply and joined Mansingh in the lobby.

"Everything all right?" he asked quietly.

She nodded. "My hair is untouched," she said as they followed the signs and the flow of people to the Arts for All event.

The room was filled with the rich and famous, many of whom were unknown to Indy, but Mansingh pointed out the Bollywood film stars, marvelling that she knew so little about his world of cinema. A waiter passed with a tray of champagne glasses and they received them gratefully.

"I think I need this," Indy said, taking an enthusiastic gulp.

"Take it easy," Mansingh cautioned and she smiled, taking another swig with a laugh.

"I'm fine. Really. I'm half Scottish and it will take more than a couple of glasses of champagne to floor me."

A man appeared by Indy's side. He was tall with thick dark hair swept back and oiled perfectly into place with not an unruly hair in sight. His beard was clipped short and trimmed into sharp angles, giving his face and jawline sculpted definition. He wore a peacock blue Nehru-style jacket over balloon-shaped trousers, which looked so surprising Indy could only imagine the outfit was made by a famous designer and had cost him a fortune.

"Excuse me," he said, placing one hand over his heart and bowing slightly. "Do I have the honour of addressing Indira

Monroe aka Detective Inspector McKinley?"

Indy smiled and held out her hand in greeting.

"My name is Shekar Bhatt, film director. Can I tell you how much I love your work."

As they continued the conversation, Mansingh excused himself, telling Indy he would be back shortly. Sheker Bhatt reached into his breast pocket and held out a card.

"May I ask you if you would be interested in appearing in one of my movies? I would be so delighted. I feel sure that our love of peacock blue is no coincidence and take it as an omen that we were meant to work together."

Indy's expression remained inscrutable as she answered, "Thank you so much." She held her hands out in a gesture of apology. "I am sorry, I don't have a card on me. But I will email you the name of my agent and we can discuss it further." Shekar returned his hand to his heart, bowing slightly, and retreated into the crowd.

Indy smiled to herself, wondering what Mr Bhatt's movies were like. She made a mental note to look him up and to educate herself on Indian cinema generally.

An amplified female voice resonated loudly and Indy turned her gaze to the woman standing on the raised dais at the end of the room, dressed in a shimmering green skirt that fell full and wide from the waist to the floor, trimmed with gold. Her top was fitted to show her full breasts off to advantage, the neckline low to display the fabulous large gold necklace that hung above her décolletage. Her black hair fell in thick waves around her very beautiful face with its perfect maquillage, large gold earrings framing the visage, and she raised her arms in greeting.

"Welcome to this very special evening in aid of the arts, something we all hold close to our hearts. How can we live without it? It is as important as food and water and this evening is about making it available to everyone. Arts for All…"

As she continued, Indy's eyes scanned the room in search of Mansingh. She saw him weaving his way through the crowd towards her, arriving with a fresh glass of champagne and an apologetic smile.

"I am sorry to leave you," he whispered, then glanced at the stage. "Ashwarya Rai, super famous actress." He glanced towards her. "You have heard of her?"

Indy nodded, sighing with relief. "Yes! *Bride and Prejudice*," she answered, aware that Mansingh looked singularly unimpressed by the reference.

Ashwarya came to the end of her speech, and then introduced, "Our host for the evening. The generous supporter of the arts, Ajay Bhatwedekar."

Indy's eyes strained to get a good look at the man who walked onto the dais. He was large and imposing, exuding wealth, power and confidence. He was dressed in a well-cut dark green suit beneath which could be seen a bright yellow shirt and a boldly patterned orange and gold tie. His hair was dyed black as was the case with most of the people of a certain age, both men and women, in the room.

"Welcome to you all, and thank you so much for supporting this cause, Arts for All. Thank you to the fabulous Ashwarya Rai for bringing such beauty to this room and introducing this very special cause so eloquently. There is little more for me to say except to please dig deep into your wallets tonight and let's make sure that we, in India, continue our tradition of creating the best arts in the world!"

There was a rousing cheer and great applause as Ajay Bhatwedekar stood with his fist raised, legs wide apart like a triumphant general about to lead his forces into battle. As he lowered his arm and walked off the stage, the applause subsided and the sound of voices in conversation and laughter resumed. Waiters with trays of napkins and edible delicacies passed by regularly and Indy accepted them eagerly, relishing the different tastes. She and Mansingh meandered through the crowd, Indy's eyes searching for an opportunity to approach her host. She did not go unrecognised. As the evening progressed and people became more relaxed, they were keen to show how knowledgeable they were of a British celebrity and with Mansingh's assistance, Indy did not appear too ignorant, much to her relief. He introduced them by name, slipping relevant references into conversation, guiding Indy smoothly.

"Indira Monroe, I believe?" The deep gravelly voice came from the imposing man who stood before her, one hand in his pocket. Ajay Bhatwedekar. Indy smiled, inclining her head to one side in confirmation, her hand fluttering subconsciously to her hair.

"How are you enjoying the evening?" he asked courteously.

Indy complimented him, mentioning the food and champagne as well as emphasising the worthy cause and she thanked him for the invitation.

Ajay grunted as though it was to be expected, his eyes scanning her with appreciation. He reached his hand to touch her elbow, guiding her to follow him as he said, "Perhaps I can show you round?"

Indy glanced towards Mansingh and saw him give an imperceptible nod and she steeled herself, feeling the man's iron grip on her arm.

"We would love to," she answered, including Mansingh in the group. "Can I introduce Mansingh Varma? He is the reason I am at this event. He works at NIT, which I believe is a college that you sponsor?"

"One of the colleges I sponsor," Ajay corrected. He looked at Mansingh. *"Calo,"* he commanded and led them out of the throng, exiting the room into the main foyer. The decor was grand, with a fountain in the centre that emitted the soft tinkle of water, bringing a sense of peace in contrast to the room they had just left with its heightened chatter of conversation. Ajay directed Indy to admire the paintings on the walls and showed off the grandeur of the enormous chandelier that hung above their heads, finally opening a door into what looked like a study.

"Welcome," he said. "Let me get you a drink… Champagne? Or will you join me in my favourite drink from your own Scottish country; whisky?"

"How can I turn down a Scots whisky?" she said. He looked at Mansingh who responded with a shake of the head.

Ajay pressed a buzzer, delivered the order and a man arrived carrying a small tray with two tumblers filled with golden liquid.

"Ice?" he asked.

Indy shook her head. "Just a splash of water," she answered.

She raised the glass to her nose inhaling the scent, then took a sip, nodding appreciatively. "Benromach?" she asked, amazed.

Ajay smiled broadly. "You know your whiskies!" he said with admiration.

Indy took another sip. "Balvenie is from Speyside, and the distillery is near my village. It makes me feel homesick just tasting it."

"So what brings you to India?" Ajay asked, settling into an armchair, spreading his legs widely. If he had been a woman, Indy thought, the position would have been beneficial for obtaining a full anatomical display of the vagina. She raised her

213

eyes from his crotch to his face and answered.

"My Netflix detective series has come to an end for the moment and I thought I would explore India. I've never been before. And you? What do you do for a living?"

He shifted his not inconsiderable body and replied, "I'm in property, my dear. This is one of my hotels. I have property in India and abroad. But let's not talk about me, I want to hear about you. What have you been doing with yourself while you've been in India?"

Indy smiled and crossed her legs, revealing a length of bare flesh beneath the side split in her dress. She watched Ajay's eyes scan her limbs and saw him inadvertently lick his lips. "Oh, I am sure you must be more interesting than I am," she said smoothly. "I believe you do a lot of travelling?"

Ajay's eyes darkened. "Of course. Why do you ask?"

Indy threw him her most winning smile. "I made the acquaintance of the most lovely flight attendant when I was flying with Qatar Airlines. I met up with her recently and I happened to mention I was coming to Arts for All tonight. I was so excited and I mentioned your name. She told me that she sometimes has the pleasure of looking after you when you travel."

Ajay shifted his seat.

"Really? What was her name?"

Indy kicked off her shoes, tucking her legs up beside her and answered thoughtfully, "Let me see… Palek…? Puneeta…? Oh, yes, I know, Priya." She looked at him to gauge a response, but there was barely a flicker of recognition in his eyes. She continued, "She was a good friend of the flight attendant who was murdered recently in Antwerp."

Ajay's jaw clenched and his eyes never left her face.

214

"Did you know her?" Indy asked. She unfolded her legs and stretched them out in front of her, sitting squarely in the armchair to face him.

He shrugged. "I am not very interested in flight attendants." He growled.

Indy leant forwards provocatively. "Really? I'm surprised. I would say you have an eye for women and flight attendants are quite gorgeous."

Ajay's fingers played with his glass and he swigged the remains of his whisky.

"Would you like another?" he asked.

Indy pondered, then asked, "Do you have Lagavulin?"

Ajay moved to the buzzer and made the order, his eyes never leaving her. "You are an intriguing woman," he said.

"Thank you, Mr Bhatwedekar, I will take that as a compliment."

The door opened and two whiskies arrived, the waiter efficiently removing the empty tumblers. He deposited a couple of dishes of nuts and crisps, bowed and left.

"Slainte mhath," Indy said, raising her glass. Ajay looked at her quizzically.

"Cheers," she translated.

Ajay raised his glass in response.

"So, seriously," Indy continued, "you're telling me you don't get to know the pretty flight attendants when you are travelling? I mean, they are waiting on your every need hand and foot for hours on end, aren't they?" She leaned back in her chair. "You're not married, are you?"

Ajay swirled the whisky in his tumbler.

"You seem very interested in my love life," he commented. "Why?"

"Why not," she answered. "It's not often I get to meet a multi-millionaire and gain an insight into his life. I'm a naturally curious person."

'You're a very beautiful woman." He turned to Mansingh with a smile. "You don't mind me saying that, do you?"

Mansingh's eyes flickered from Indy to Ajay and he cleared his throat. "Not at all. I agree with you."

Indy smiled.

"There are two things I love in this world; one is acting" – she smiled at him – "and the other is diamonds." Ajay's eyes narrowed. "I was married once, but it didn't work out. Sometimes, I wonder if it was because he never bought me a diamond ring." She looked up at him. "What do you think?"

He moved towards her. "I think you would look gorgeous in diamonds," he stated.

Indy sat up slightly. "Do you?" she asked brightly. "What sort of diamonds would look good on me?"

Ajay had closed in on her now, and he stood in front of her, with his legs astride her. "I think you are not only a beautiful woman, but a clever one. You want to know about diamonds? I'll tell you about them. If you were with me, I would give you pink diamonds and blue diamonds. Yellow diamonds and sapphire ones. You would wear them around your throat and on your fingers. On your ears and on your feet. I could bury you in diamonds."

Indy felt her heart pounding as the blood rushed through her veins. "That's a lot of diamonds," she said. "Where would you find them all?"

Ajay leaned over her, his face close to hers. "I have more diamonds than you can imagine," he said.

Indy needed all her powers to remain calm as she asked,

216

"Where do you get all your diamonds?"

"I think you know very well where I get them. I buy them from South Africa and Zimbabwe."

"Aren't they what's called blood diamonds?" she asked.

Ajay let out a blast of mirthless laughter. "Blood diamonds... Look around you, woman. People complain about the conditions of the diamond mines. What about the people on our streets? Self-righteous customers demand a conflict-free certificate so they can justify their purchases. But certificates are so easy to get. All you need is some money for a bribe and anyone will sign anything. Just like that. People know this in their hearts, they just turn a blind eye to it. Just as they turn a blind eye to the poverty on our streets. I should know, I was brought up in the slums. But I got myself out. I have earned my money."

He looked at her. "You think you are clever, but you are not clever enough. I have you underneath me and there is nothing you can do about it."

Indy's eyes bored into his. "Are you going to kill me as you killed Arundhati? She was smuggling diamonds for you, wasn't she?"

Ajay growled. "Yes, she was, but she was becoming too demanding. She wanted too much and I was getting tired of her." He stood over her, looking down on her, revelling in his power. "It was good while it lasted. She was a very good lay" – his eyes scanned her body – "and by the looks of things, you would be too." He turned to look at Mansingh. "Is she, Mansingh?"

Indy looked over at Mansingh, and was puzzled at his response. "She's OK," he answered nonchalantly.

Ajay laughed and Indy jerked her knee upwards, hitting his crotch hard. His hands rushed to his groin and he fell to his knees in agony and surprise. She drew in her feet and kicked him hard in the chest, and he reeled backwards.

"Mansingh," he called out in a hoarse whisper.

Indy stared at Mansingh. "Why is he calling your name?" she asked, a hard edge to her voice.

Mansingh moved towards her and then knelt down over Ajay, pulling cable ties out of his trousers. Indy looked at him quizzically.

"They don't show up in the security check," he said with a shrug.

Ajay's eyes widened in disbelief. "Mansingh?" he asked. "What are you doing?" He let out a growl of rage as he grabbed onto Mansingh's throat, kicking his legs in an effort to raise himself. Indy grabbed Ajay by the balls and saw his grip loosen just enough to allow Mansingh to bring his hands in between his opponent's arms, forcing them apart.

He threw a couple of cable ties towards Indy and she bound his legs while Mansingh secured Ajay's arms behind him. Indy reached into her cleavage and pulled out a small pouch, dangling it above Ajay's face.

"Oh, by the way, I believe you are missing some diamonds, is that right?"

Ajay nodded. She continued, "Sorry, I didn't quite catch that. You've got people looking for them quite aggressively, I believe; beating them up, assaulting them, haven't you? Well, haven't you?"

"What if I have?" he growled.

"Have you?" Indy persisted.

"Yes," he barked at her.

She smiled. "I thought so. Well, I meant to say that I found your missing diamonds. The ones you've been looking so hard for. The ones Arundhati smuggled for you. Maybe all you had to do was to ask nicely." She laughed harshly.

Ajay let out a loud roar as he wriggled forcefully on the floor.

"You were like a son to me, Mansingh. Why are you doing this? She's just an actress – they are two a penny. I can get you any number of actresses for your pleasure," he said, twisting his eyes to meet Mansingh's, who replied with a smile.

"You have one or two of your fingers in Bollywood pies, don't you? You are a major financier of films... Who can you get for me...?"

Ajay replied eagerly, "Who do you want? I will get her – or them..."

Mansingh continued in a sincere voice, "What if I want someone murdered, will you do that for me too? I've been having some financial problems."

Indy looked at him, suddenly unsure if he was going to do a deal with this man.

"You need money? You should have told me. Who has been bothering you? I will have them dealt with immediately."

Mansingh persisted, "Dealt with? Or murdered. I want them to feel the pain, I want them to suffer slowly before they die."

Ajay was sweating. "Yes, yes! Free me and I will make it happen. Whatever you need, just let me go."

Mansingh laughed and said, "As if you would let me go after this, Ajay. Do you take me for a fool?"

At this, Ajay's rage exploded and Mansingh threw himself over Ajay's mouth to quieten him and said loudly, "Code Indigo, Code Indigo," while Indy looked at him confused. "Your dupatta. We need to shut him up."

Ajay was roaring loudly while Indy was attempting to stuff the fabric in his mouth when the door was flung open by Jitu and Vasant. They looked temporarily relieved as they saw Mansingh in the room then their eyes took in Ajay lying trussed up like a chicken on the floor and they reached for their guns. Ajay was turning purple with rage as he struggled on the floor.

Mansingh and Indy made a dive behind the armchairs, their eyes searching desperately for something to use as a weapon.

Jitu looked from his boss to the armchairs and then to Vasant.

"He looks pretty angry," he said. "Shall I untie him first?" Ajay's muffled sounds reached a pitch of exasperation at the question.

Vasant nodded, his outstretched arms holding his gun in front of him as he moved towards the chair while Jitu lowered his weapon and knelt beside Ajay.

"You might as well show yourselves," Vasant said. "There's nowhere you can go."

Cautiously, he moved around the back of the chair when suddenly, Mansingh made a dive towards Vasant's legs unbalancing him while Indy high kicked the gun out of his hands. She felt her dress rip in response to the movement.

"Damn," she said. "I really liked this dress."

Mansingh smiled. "I'll get you another one—watch out!"

She reeled around with a leap, whipping her leg out as she turned in time to fling Jitu onto his side where he landed hard on top of Ajay.

"Put your hands behind your heads and lie on the floor," came the command. A group of heavily armed men stood in the doorway, their guns pointing straight at the pair.

Indy's jaw dropped. "What the…" she uttered as she obediently moved her hands as ordered.

"I'm undercover. Code Indigo," he said.

Indy turned to stare at him. "You're what?" she gasped.

"I'll tell you about it later." He pointed to Ajay. "Ajay

Bhatwedekar, the boss of the organisation." He waved his arm over Jitu and Vasant. "And those two are with him." Sweat trickled down his face. "Is it OK if I wipe my face?"

A man with a thick moustache emerged between the armed men and nodded and Mansingh reached into his breast pocket, pulling out a handkerchief.

"My father told me never to leave the house without one. It was the best advice he ever gave me," he said as he mopped his face and neck.

The man walked towards Mansingh, holding out his hand.

"Well done," he said, clapping him on the back. "This has been a long time coming." He turned to Indy. "And I believe we've got you to thank for obtaining the evidence? We have been after Ajay Bhatwedekar for a long, long time, not just for diamond smuggling, but for extortion, film finance and several murders."

Indy looked from one man to the other. "I don't understand..." she said.

The man with the moustache answered, "Ajay Bhatwedekar was known to us, but we needed hard evidence and until tonight, Ajay was a careful man. Mansingh worked hard to gain his trust, but we could never get the incriminating evidence we needed to convict him. Ajay was always careful to only talk openly about his plans while in one of his homes where he was protected by Faraday cages. And then you came along. Who would have thought you would get the better of Ajay Bhatwedekar." He looked at the large body bound and apoplectic on the carpet. "Not Ajay, it seems."

Mansingh felt his body fatigue. "Permission to leave?" he asked.

The chief nodded, then turned to Indy. "May I?" he asked,

his hand outstretched.

Indy looked at him blankly for a moment, then reached into her hair and pulled out the recording device and placed it in the palm of his hand.

His fingers closed over it. "I love modern technology." He smiled. "Wires are so hard to detect these days." He turned towards Ajay. "Who would have thought it, *eh*, Ajay?" He spun round with authority to his team. "*Okay!* Let's get this scum out of here."

Chapter 30
Mumbai 2018

Indy opened the curtains and gazed out of the hotel bedroom window. The day looked just like any other day. The sun was shining and people were going about their business as usual. It was hard to believe the events of last night, though she could feel the bruising on her body. She looked behind her at the man lying in bed and watched him stir, peeling open his eyelids that were resistant to the light streaming in from the parted curtains. He eased himself up onto the pillows and looked at her.

"Are you OK?" he asked.

Indy nodded and turned back to watch the Mumbai morning.

Mansingh stretched, yawning loudly. "I'm hungry," he stated. "Let's get some breakfast and then I probably need to go into the office and make my report. But I should be free this evening. What would you like to do?"

Indy turned back to look at him. "I don't even know who you are," she said. "All that time we spent together, you were lying. What were you doing with me? You were using me to get information on Ajay, and yet you were working for him. How can I believe anything you said to me?"

Mansingh's jaw clenched and he reached out to her.

"Everything between us has been real, Indy. You must believe that. I couldn't tell you what I was doing, my life depended on Ajay trusting me and it would have been dangerous for you to know. You had to go to the party last night just as you are, with no secrets. Don't you see? If Ajay had had one whiff of betrayal, we would have died."

She looked at him speaking to her so earnestly and said, "I want to trust you, Mansingh. But now I know how good an actor you are – you might be even better than me, I don't know…" she laughed mirthlessly.

Indy sat on the end of the bed, out of his reach.

"There are some things I don't understand," she said. "Who was the man with the tattoo on his arm? Was he working for Ajay? Was Ajay having me followed?"

Mansingh smiled ruefully. "His name is Ajanta and he works for me. I had him follow you for your protection, just in case. There was a bit of a problem when Priya was attacked by Ajay's thugs."

Indy gasped at this information, "Oh no! Was that why she didn't meet me at the Mirror Market?"

Mansingh nodded. "Luckily, Ajanta was there, waiting for you to arrive and he stepped in."

She shuddered. "Poor Priya. It was my fault."

"No, it was Ajay's fault. He was looking for the diamonds and thought Priya might know something. You mustn't blame yourself." He smiled at Indy. "Of course, he was furious that Jitu and Vasant were found tied up in the Law Gardens by a passerby so he asked me to track Ajanta down." Mansingh laughed. "That was easy enough to do, of course. I sent him a photo of Ajanta looking beautifully murdered with my compliments." Mansingh was grinning and Indy struggled to reconcile this man with the kind, thoughtful IT person she thought she had fallen in love with.

"What I still don't know," he continued, "is who killed Arundhati." His eyes searched Indy's face in an effort to gauge her response. "That was a shame. Ajay had sent me to kill her."

At these words, Indy's eyes widened.

"Which, of course, I wasn't going to do. We had a witness protection plan in place for her, but she decided to steal those diamonds and complicate the matter." He paused, then said, "I saw you there, you know."

Indy returned his gaze.

"You took a phone out of the bin, just outside Arundhati's hotel. I passed you, don't you remember?"

Indy reached back into her memory and found the moment she had first seen the man she would have an affair with.

"I remember. You bumped into me."

"It seems I'm not the only one good at keeping secrets." He smiled. "You never told me you were in Antwerp, did you?"

Indy shrugged.

He continued, "It doesn't matter. But if I, that is to say, Ajay, didn't kill her – and you didn't kill her – then who did?" His eyes bored into hers and Indy looked away.

He nodded, accepting her silence.

"So what do we do now?" he asked her.

Indy inhaled deeply, letting out an audible sigh.

"I don't know, Mansingh," she said. "Give me some time to get used to the new you. I've got something I need to do. It will take me away from Mumbai. Let's see where the dust settles." At these words, Mansingh closed his eyes, then threw off the sheet and got out of bed.

Wordlessly, he dressed and left the room without looking back. Indy watched him go and felt an emptiness inside.

Calicut 2018

Indy's taxi pulled up outside Sonal and Prakash's house. She had

225

phoned before leaving Mumbai to say that she wanted to see the couple one last time before leaving India and had sensed a change in Sonal's manner towards her. A lot had happened since they had last seen each other and in many ways, Indy was not surprised. People don't always like others seeing their dirty laundry, even when they have asked them to wash it.

Sonal opened the door and invited Indy inside, bringing her into the living room to meet her mother-in-law. Prakash was there too, his arm in a sling, the signs of bruising still apparent. They sat and made the usual exchanges of casual conversation while coffee was brought and then Indy said, "I wonder if we could have a word in private." She looked at Sonal and then Prakash, who nodded and turned to his mother with a nod of his head.

"Ma? Could you give us a moment," he pleaded. "Just a short time, we won't be long."

His mother looked from one to the other, then made a gesture of exasperation before heaving herself off the sofa and exiting the room.

Indy turned to Sonal and Prakash.

"You will have heard on the news that Ajay Bhatwedekar, the man responsible for having you beaten up, is in custody," she stated and they nodded.

"It's not up to me, but I don't see any reason to involve you both in the investigation. I never told anyone where the diamonds came from." She saw Sonal's expression change from one of relief to worry as she turned to look at her husband. He looked at them both in astonishment and asked, "Diamonds?"

Indy looked at Sonal and asked, "Where did you find the diamonds, Sonal?"

Sonal avoided eye contact and muttered, "I went to your flat, Prakash. I was mad with jealousy so when you went to Antwerp,

226

I thought I would look for proof of your affair with that woman. When I found that you had given her my locket – the locket that you had given *me* as a present – I went crazy. I took the locket and turned your flat upside down. Later on, I found out by accident that she had hidden the diamonds inside the locket."

Prakash was staring at her, his jaw dropped in amazement and he stuttered, "They kept asking me over and over if I knew where they were… but I didn't know… I didn't know…"

Indy nodded. "Maybe it was best that you didn't," she said. "So, it was you who ransacked the flat, Sonal. I thought it might have been when you lied to me about having stayed at home. I knew you had been at an airport because your phone made a pocket call to me."

She watched Sonal's guilty expression with some satisfaction and then shifted her focus back to Prakash.

"And they don't know that you were at Arundhati's hotel in Antwerp when she was killed," she said.

His jaw dropped and he paled at her words. "You were there? But how? Why?"

Sonal stared at the floor in silence.

"Prakash, I saw you go into her hotel, and I saw you leave. I also saw you drop her phone into the bin outside the flat. I rescued it."

Sonal gasped, gathering her dupatta to her mouth to stifle the sound. Indira looked at them both.

"Sonal wanted me to find out if you were still having an affair with Arundhati. She was desperate, so I agreed. I followed you to Antwerp and" – she paused – "I have to know. Did you kill Arundhati?"

At these words, Sonal could not contain her sobs.

Prakash's eyes swivelled wildly between the two women and

227

then he crumpled, nodding.

"I didn't go there to kill her. I went to talk to her. I thought she was seeing someone else, but I needed to know for sure. I was going to finish it there and then... put an end to the relationship, I mean, but she taunted me. She told me she was going to be rich, that she had been having an affair with someone much more important than me. She went on and on and I couldn't stand it any more. I didn't mean to kill her. We got into a fight and I pushed her hard. She fell backwards on the coffee table and hit her head. I didn't know what to do. I couldn't have anyone knowing that I was with her." He turned to Sonal, pleading, "I couldn't have you knowing..." Then he turned back to look at Indy. "She was dead. I know she was dead. There was blood coming out of her head, blood everywhere and she wasn't breathing..." He closed his eyes and cried.

Indy nodded. Sonal looked at Indy. "What are you going to do? You're not going to tell the police, are you?" she beseeched.

Indy shook her head.

"No, I'm not going to tell the police. I'm not going to tell anyone." She rose from her chair and looked at them both.

"Be kind to each other," she said.

Indy walked out of the house and took a deep breath. Maybe holidays were overrated, she thought.

Epilogue

Indy's suitcase lay open on the bed, bulging with the contents, but optimistically ready to close. She had spent the last couple of days shopping on her own, with a list of friends and family to buy presents for, clutched in her hand. It was a pleasure to have nothing else organised; nobody to see, nothing else to do…and no murders to solve. She closed the suitcase, leaning on it heavily as she persuaded the reluctant zip to bring the top and bottom together. It was time to go home. She closed her eyes and saw her mother's image and her thoughts returned to the reunion with her grandparents. Her eyes welled up with tears and she wiped them away from the corners of her eyes. She sighed deeply and pulled out her phone, opening her photos, scrolling back to the day she met them for the very first time. There she was, looming between the much smaller figures of her Dadi and Dada, her arms around their shoulders. She smiled at the sight of them and her stomach gave a flutter at the thought of what her Mother would feel seeing them after all these years when she showed her their photo.

Indy scanned the room one last time and satisfied that she had left nothing behind she closed the door behind her.

Sandeep was waiting for her by his padmini, ready to take her suitcase and open the door for her as if she were royalty. On seeing her his face lit up with a smile and she noted the familiar waggle of the head. She would miss him, she thought.

As she stepped out of the car at the airport she took one last deep inhalation, closing her eyes to absorb and embed the smells and sounds of India deep within her.

"You will be back, Indy?" Sandeep said.

Indy smiled and answered his question with a fair imitation of a bobble of the head.

"Of course," she replied, giving him a big hug, and saw him grin with delight.

She stepped into the airport; that place that bridges cultures without offering any of its own. A no-man's land of transitions, and she knew she was ready. Ready to return to the rain, to the wind, to the grey skies, fresh air, the woods of Forres and the beaches of Nairn.

Indy settled into her seat on the plane while the woman next to her buckled her seatbelt and pulled the strap tighter, accidentally elbowing Indy in the ribs.

"Oh, I'm sorry," she said apologetically, turning towards Indy. The blue eyes scanned Indy's face thoughtfully, and then flickered as recognition hit her.

"D I McKinley!" she exclaimed. "Well I never! I'm such a fan." Her face was bathed in delight. Then she leaned towards Indy, lowering her voice conspiratorially and said, "tell me, have you been travelling on business or pleasure?"

A wan smile flickered over Indy's lips and she closed her eyes. This was going to be a long flight home, she thought.

The End